no way out but up

AN ANGEL ROMANTIC COMEDY

CECIL LATWINE

KNOWHERE MEDIA

For Robert, my guardian angel in real life.

*And a special thank you to my friend, Danny, for his wonderful
creative mind.*

one

Elsie

Everything about the walkway up to my front door was perfect. Grass mowed and edged along the brick pathway. Flower beds weeded leaving the purple, pink, and white tulips to flourish. Stone steps power washed. Not a speck of dirt or gravel in sight.

Perfect.

I loved my landscape company. They always came on the same day as my cleaning service. I scheduled them that way so at least one day a week I arrived home to ideal conditions. They never left anything out of place. Just the way I liked it.

Which was why I found it strange the day I slipped my key into my front door and heard a thumping sound coming from inside.

An erratic muffled thumping, rather like the sound of a bird fluttering up against a window when they are stuck in a house trying to escape. Had the cleaning service inadvertently let a bird into my house?

I pushed the door open and the scent of newly applied lemon

oil greeted me. Refreshing. But the thumping persisted. I zeroed in on the sound. It was coming from the kitchen.

I quietly hung my keys on my key hook and placed my purse in its assigned drawer in the pine side board, but kept my shoes on just in case I had to chase a wild bird out of my kitchen. I opened the coat closet as quietly as possible and retrieved my precision angle bristle broom in case I needed to swat at the thing.

As I moved silently down the hallway to my kitchen the thumping grew more frantic. And louder. Must be a large bird.

Nervous, I've never been good with animals, I paused at the kitchen doorway and got a good grip on the handle. Holding the business end of the broom in front of me, just slightly above my head to keep the bird from getting tangled up in my hair, I stepped around the corner and flipped on the light.

There were feathers everywhere. Huge white feathers floating in the air, stuck to the walls, and tumbling lightly across the tile floor. The feathers, however, were not what stopped me in my tracks.

It was the man. A man – not a bird – was in my kitchen.

And he wasn't flying up against the window trying to get out. He was hanging from the ceiling fan.

Not hanging. *Hanging.* As in *from his neck*!

"Oh my God, oh my God!" I screamed.

The hanging man flopped uncontrollably. The giant costume wings he wore on his back were so wide that as he flopped they bumped against the wall, making the thumping sound I had heard.

"Oh my God!" I screamed again. Nobody else was there. I lived alone. I had no time to think, something had to be done.

I dropped the broom and rushed to him. I was eye level with his blue jean clad thighs so I grabbed them tight and hoisted up. I heard a thin whine as he gasped for air.

I screamed again. This time there were no words, just fear and frustration. He was heavy. But I dug deep for strength, bent my knees, and managed to push him up a little further.

Another gasp. Thank God!

And a snap. Then a crack.

Pieces of plaster fell past me, some of them sticking to my nose. There must have been dust, because suddenly I needed to cough. When I inhaled, some of the plaster dust went to the back of my throat causing me to gag and cough at the same time.

I coughed so hard my grip on the man's legs failed and I felt him slip. I heard another snapping sound. I looked up into the glare of my kitchen ceiling fan and saw the rope holding him was tied to the light fixture. And the light fixture was about to fall.

two

Elsie

When he fell, I crumpled to the floor under his crushing weight.

I had never had a grown man fall on top of me, but it seemed like this one was extremely heavy. And awkward. I ended up like a cartoon character squished underneath him with my limbs splayed out in all directions.

"Mm-rr-ph," I screamed into his flannel shirt, which was pressed against my mouth. But he didn't budge.

For a split second I was terrified he was dead and I was to remain trapped under him until next week when my cleaning service let themselves in. By then we would both be dead. And with no explanation to my friends and family about who the person was who flattened me.

He gasped. A full gasp this time, not the thin-nearly-choked-to-death gasp from earlier.

He was alive!

Now to get him off of me.

"Mm-rr-ph!" I screamed again and wiggled the only parts of me that weren't held down. My arms and legs.

He was breathing at least. His flannel shirt was heaving in and out against my face. I could hear his heartbeat. My face must have been directly underneath his chest.

"Mm-rr-ph!" I tried again. This time there was a reaction. "Wha–?"

The flannel shirt shifted. There was grunting. Mine and his.

Finally he moved far enough to the side that my mouth was free.

"Move!" I yelled, gasping for breath now that he had almost smothered me with his massive lumberjack bulk.

"Wait. What?" He was confused. I guess I couldn't blame him. He had just had a near death experience. But still, my arms and legs were going numb.

"Get. Off. Of. Me." I said with as much command as someone can when they're squashed like a bug.

"Oh no, oh no, oh no," he repeated with more and more desperation as he clamored off of my body, only kneeing me twice with too much severity in the process.

As soon as I was mobile I scrambled up off the floor and got my first good look at him.

Not as hulking as I would have thought, given how it had felt when I was underneath him. Dead weight is a real thing, I guess.

Brown hair, 30-ish, flannel shirt, jeans, brown boots, that would all be expected with the flannel look. What wasn't expected were the giant costume wings he wore on his back. The source of both the massive amount of loose plumage flying around my kitchen and the great confusion on my part.

"Who in the hell are you?" I asked.

The guy's mouth fell open as if I had just appeared out of thin air and yelled at him. He pushed against the wall, getting leverage to stand. This was made especially difficult because he still had a rope tied around his neck, which was tethered to my kitchen ceiling fan. The ceiling fan light fixture that now lay broken on the floor between us.

As he stood I could see that he wasn't exactly a small guy. Not bone crushing huge, but still about six feet tall and meaty enough. I eyed my broom on the floor, which I had discarded when I raced to his rescue.

"Listen," I said, using my commanding voice again. "I don't know what's going on here or how you ended up in my kitchen, but who in the hell *are* you and what in the hell are you doing *here*?"

Standing with his back leaning against the wall, goofy costume wings sticking out from behind him, he touched his stomach then his chest then his face. Completely dumbfounded.

I was losing patience. "Look, I don't want to call the police if you're in trouble or something, but I will if you don't tell me what's going on."

Completely bewildered, the guy stared at me with eyes all big and wide and scared, and asked, "You-you can see me?"

three

Elsie

"Of course I can see you," I spat out the words before I had a moment to think.

Then I did think.

Cold fear shot down my spine.

He was crazy. Or, even worse, he was on something, tripping in my kitchen, trying to hang himself. Or, maybe, someone else tried to hang this guy in my kitchen.

It hadn't even occurred to me until that point that he may not be the only intruder in my home. What if there was a whole gang of them wandering around my house wearing disturbingly comedic costumes and doing inexplicable things to one another?

Angel Boy was still flabbergasted at the fact that I could see him. It was written all over his unhinged eyes.

"Th-that's impossible," he stammered.

I decided to take on the adult role in the situation. I just had to act like I did when I babysat my niece and nephew.

"It's entirely possible for me to see you because you are

standing right here in *my* kitchen." I pointed at the floor for emphasis.

"Not good, not good, not good," the guy raised his eyes to the ceiling then dropped his face into his hands. "What did I do?"

With a rush of relief, I remembered that I had my cell in my pocket. Fishing it out I swiped it open to the phone app. He dropped his hands to his sides despondently and watched me.

"I'm just gonna get you some help, okay?"

"Don't do that Elsie," he said.

Another shot of fear zipped through my body.

"How do you know my name?"

His shoulders slumped, as if he had made yet another mistake in a long line of mistakes. "I'm sorry, I'm not trying to scare you."

"I'm not scared," I lied.

"I can explain," he said, pushing off the wall and walking toward me.

"Stay back!" I held up my palm like I was a traffic cop.

He stopped, but all of his movement disturbed the mass of loose feathers in the room. A cloud of them floated halfway up his legs then fluttered down again.

I kept my eyes on him and my traffic cop palm facing him. I used the thumb on my hand holding my phone to hit 9-1-1 then Send.

"You just called 9-1-1 didn't you?" he asked, defeated.

"No," I lied again.

He sighed and went to throw his face into his hands when one hand got tangled up in the rope that still hung from his neck. He looked down at it, almost surprised it was there. He tugged at it and when it didn't come off right away he grabbed at the noose around his throat and pulled harder. With growing agitation he turned and yanked the noose until it finally loosened enough for him to pull it off over his head. He let it drop to the floor.

"9-1-1 what's your emergency," a voice said on the other end of the phone.

"Tell them it was a mistake," he said.

I hit speaker on my phone so they could hear everything that went on.

"My name is Elsie Martin and there's an intruder in my house."

Angel Boy shook his head. "They're not going to be able to see me."

I rolled my eyes.

"What's the address?" 9-1-1 asked.

I gave them my address while Angel Boy looked down at the feathers at his feet, disheartened by my actions.

"I think he's on drugs or something. And he-he has a rope," I told the operator.

He looked up at me, a little hurt by my report.

"A rope?" the operator asked.

"Yes."

"Is he still in the building?"

"Yes! He's standing right in front of me," I said.

"They can't hear me either," Angel Boy said.

I scoffed at him. "I doubt it. I have this on speaker. So you better not do anything you don't want the police to record."

"Ma'am, are you okay?"

"No, I'm not okay! There's an intruder in my house dressed like a-" I flicked my eyes over the span of his giant white costume wings. "An angel." I gave him a questioning look.

He shrugged and nodded. "A guardian angel," he said bitterly.

"Dressed like a guardian angel," I repeated.

"You think he's dressed as a *guardian* angel...specifically?" The operator asked.

"I don't think that. He just said so. Didn't you hear him?"

"I did not," the operator replied with, I thought, a little bit of attitude. "We have people on the way. I'm going to stay on the phone with you until the officers get there."

"Okay, thank you," I said, relieved that soon the authorities would arrive.

Angel Boy was watching me with concern. "Would you feel safer if I sat down?"

"Yes, on the floor," I answered.

"Okay," he turned around to go back to where he'd sat against the wall before standing. His wing whipped around when he turned and hit my hand. My cell phone went flying across the kitchen and headed for the wall.

I cried out and lunged for it, certain he would grab it first and convince the 9-1-1 operator that I had called as a bad joke.

Just before the phone hit the wall it stopped. Just stopped. Frozen in mid-air.

I stopped too. I thought I was imagining it, but then I took a breath. Then another. And the phone still hung there, the timer still clicking forward on the call.

I stepped in front of the phone, marveling at it, not believing my eyes.

"Ma'am, are you still there?" The operator's voice came through clear as could be.

"Ye–" my voice cracked. I cleared my throat. "Yes, I'm still here."

I turned my eyes ever so slowly toward Angel Boy sitting against my kitchen wall. He locked eyes with me and gave me an apologetic smile.

"The police are at your door," the operator said.

I looked back at the phone dangling, no, floating right in front of my face.

"Did you hear me, ma'am? The police are at your door."

I reached out and plucked the phone out of thin air. That's when they kicked my front door in.

four

Elsie

A lot of things happened to me that night. Things I had never experienced before.

There was the whole finding an intruder in my home, saving him from death, calling 9-1-1, just a lot of things. The most humiliating by far was when the police pinned me down because they thought I was a suspect.

"What are you doing? I'm the victim! I'm the victim!" I shouted as they barreled down the hallway and threw me to the ground. For the second time that night I was splayed out on the floor under the full weight of a grown man.

Out of the corner of my eye I could see the real culprit watching and wincing as the officer pulled my arms behind my back.

"It's him, not me! He broke into my house!" I screamed.

No matter how many times I told the police about the man who was sitting right in front of them, they paid no attention to him. Even when I calmed down and they agreed to let me sit on a kitchen chair and explain why I had called 9-1-1 they didn't so much as look in his direction.

"I got home and heard a thumping sound. I thought it was a bird trapped in my kitchen," I told them.

Angel Boy watched with empathy from his seat on the floor. I avoided eye contact with him while I spoke with the police.

"And then what happened?" the oldest looking male officer who seemed to be in charge asked.

"I got my broom and came to the kitchen." I glanced quickly at Angel Boy. He looked worried. I looked back at the officer. "I turned on the lights and came in the room and he was hanging there." I pointed at the hole in my ceiling. "From that." I pointed at the broken ceiling fan on the floor.

"Who was hanging there?" The officer asked.

I slid my eyes to Angel Boy. He shook his head and said out loud, bold as can be, "Don't tell them, Elsie. They can't see me or hear me. They won't believe you."

I looked at the officers in disbelief. They were all looking at me as if he hadn't just spoken. As if he wasn't there at all.

"A man," I answered.

"Do you know the man?"

"No, I do not."

"And then what happened?" The officer asked patiently.

"I held him up because he was choking on the rope."

"He was hanging from a rope?" The officer clarified.

I nodded. "Yes, but the ceiling fan broke and he fell on top of me. The light fixture fell down into all this mess of feathers."

"What feathers?" The officer asked.

I gaped at the giant white feathers all over the floor. The same feathers that the officers were kicking around when they walked. Angel Boy shook his head as a warning.

"Um, he was wearing feathers. Wings. On his back," I said.

"Right," the older officer looked at a younger female officer. "Wasn't there something about that in the call?"

"Yes, the operator said the caller stated the intruder was dressed as an angel," she answered.

"A guardian angel," I corrected her.

The older officer gave me an odd look.

"I guess that's not really important," I mumbled.

He cleared his throat. "And what happened to the man?"

I side-eyed Angel Boy who was anxiously waiting for my answer. Then I had an idea.

"You haven't seen him? A guy wearing angel wings?" I asked the officers, giving them the chance to tell me that he was sitting right there behind them.

Again the odd look. "No, Miss, we didn't find anyone else in your house."

And that was when I knew I must have suffered a mental breakdown. Cold sweat broke out on my forehead and my heart started racing. Invisible men. Floating cell phones. There was no other explanation.

My hallucination spoke up. "Don't panic, Elsie. I can explain everything after they're gone."

I wanted more than anything to tell him to be quiet, but that wouldn't look crazy, would it? Yelling at someone who wasn't there?

I kept my wits about me long enough to answer all of the officer's questions, thank them for their help, assure them that I would call a locksmith and have them install a new lock on my now broken door immediately, and wave goodbye to them as they drove away.

When I turned around he was standing behind me. I almost ran into him and his giant wings because they were blocking the entire hallway.

"Since you are a product of my imagination, I hereby request that you take those stupid things off while I figure out what to do," I said curtly.

"My wings?" He seemed astounded. Again. Everything I said

was like a huge surprise to this guy. Strange, since he had been created in my mind. "I can't take off my wings," he said.

"And why is that?"

He lowered his gaze, almost bashful, and said, "Because I'm an angel."

I snorted out a laugh. "Right, a guardian angel."

He looked up at me, embarrassed, "Actually, Elsie, I'm *your* guardian angel."

five

Elsie

He had to help me back into the kitchen. I was shaking too hard to walk straight.

Kicking away pieces of broken ceiling fan and feathers, he led me to the same kitchen chair I had been interrogated in and turned it toward the table so I would have something to lean on.

"Can I get you a drink of water or something?" he asked.

I nodded. My mouth was dry. My head was spinning.

He brought a glass of water and placed it in front of me before going into an elaborate series of maneuvers to sit his body and his wings down at the table across from where I sat.

I sipped my water and watched him get settled. By the time he was fully seated I had stopped shaking and felt a little better.

"You all good now?" I asked, indicating his chair with a tip of my head.

"Yes, I'm in," he said. His wings stretched behind him and fluffed out, sending a few random feathers flying off.

I watched the feathers flutter through the air and land on the trashed kitchen floor.

"I'm sorry about the mess. I know how you don't like messes," he said, giving me an unhappy look.

He was right. I didn't like messes. I almost asked him how he knew that, but then I remembered he was my hallucination. Of course he would know everything about me. Maybe I needed to know more about him so I could figure out why he had suddenly materialized in my consciousness.

"Why are you losing feathers?" I asked.

He craned his neck to look over his shoulder at his wings.

I jerked my head in the direction of the floor. "I mean, is that normal for an angel? To drop feathers everywhere?"

He looked glumly at the sea of feathers surrounding them and shook his head 'no'.

"Then what's going on?"

"I may be molting."

"Molting."

He nodded, running a hand through his hair. I took a moment to look him over really well for the first time.

For an illusion he wasn't bad looking. Strange combination of the whole lumberjack look with the white angel wings, but who knew what part of my subconscious that was coming from.

Otherwise, as far as his face and build, he could be considered a good looking guy. Perhaps a little younger than I had first pegged him. Brown hair, blue eyes, or were they hazel? Either way he wasn't very scary, which was nice. I would have really freaked out if he was a frightening figment of my imagination.

Another question popped into my mind.

"If you're my guardian angel, why were you hanging in my kitchen like that? You had a noose around your neck."

He put his elbows on the table and covered his face with both hands, moaning miserably, "This is not good."

"Did somebody do that to you or..." I hesitated. The other option was pretty awful.

He separated two fingers so one eye could peek out at me.

"No," I said. "You weren't...?"

"I'm sorry," he said.

So appalled I couldn't think of what to say, I gawked at him then up at the hole in my ceiling then back at him.

"You, my guardian angel, tried to hang yourself in my kitchen!?" It was my turn to be astounded.

He reached across the table toward me then let his hands drop in defeat. "I'm so, so, so sorry."

"I don't understand. What would make you do something like that?" I asked. Truly, I wanted to know. It was a horrifying idea and it would be good for me to know what this scenario symbolized when I found a therapist. "Do I have low self-esteem or something?"

"No, it's not you, Elsie. Not exactly," he answered. He let out a heavy sigh prompting another feather to pop off the uppermost corner of his left wing. "I've been a bit...hopeless lately. Well, longer than lately. For years and years now."

"Hopeless. Why?"

He looked at me nervously. Not sure how I was going to react. I gave him an encouraging smile.

"It's just, well, you see, there's not much about you that needs guarding."

"There's not?"

"No, there's nothing, in fact. Nothing for me to help you with." He shrugged. Resigned to his fate. Seeing my surprise he added, "You're very good at guarding yourself." Then under his breath. "Excellent at it, in fact."

I was insulted at this assessment. "I don't think I'm too guarded."

He let out a course laugh, then contained it when he saw my expression. "Sorry, I'm not trying to upset you."

"What are you trying to do, Angel Boy? Coming in here uninvited and hanging yourself?" I asked, annoyed.

"It's ZakZakiel," he said quietly.

"What?"

"My name."

"You have a name?"

A little affronted, he said, "Of course I have a name. Everyone's got a name."

"And yours is Zak?"

"ZakZakiel," he annunciated carefully.

"Zak Zakiel," I repeated it as a first and last name.

"No, together. It's one word. Say it all at once, ZakZakiel."

"Whatever." This was stupid and off topic. "I'll call you Zak, how's that?"

"All right," he threw up his hands weakly like he was suffering another expected failure.

I didn't want to argue with an illusion all night. I was worn out from all of the activity and I hadn't eaten since lunch.

"Are you hungry?" Zak asked, perking up at the idea.

"A little." I eyed him, suspicious.

"I could make you something," he offered hopefully.

I should interject here that I am a dietician. A nutritionist. A person who knows exactly what should be going into ones meals for maximum benefit to ones body. Rarely have I allowed anyone else to fix my food and I am extremely picky about where I eat out.

Looking into Zak's eager eyes, which were hazel for sure, I remembered that he was me, so it didn't matter.

"Sure, why not?"

"Really?" He raised his hand to stop me from answering. "Never mind. I'll take what I can."

For the next half hour I watched in amazement as Zak flitted around my kitchen, humming to himself, fixing me a turkey avocado sandwich on sprouted wheat bread and a side of greens with balsamic dressing.

I was so impressed. Not so much with his cooking skills, because I knew they were my cooking skills, but at my amazing brain. The fact that this hallucination looked so real. Seemed so authentic. He even spilled some dressing on the front of his red and black lumberjack shirt and had to wash it off at the sink.

I was pretty proud of my brain at that point. It had amazing capabilities that had been a little sidetracked, that's all. I just needed to seek out some help in getting it back in line with reality.

"Thank you," I said as Zak placed the simple meal in front of me.

He sat down opposite me again, managing his wings better this time, and watched me eat.

"Mmm," I made sure to let him know how good it was. I was sort of having fun with my little mind game.

"You like it?" he asked, pleased.

I nodded as I chewed and studied his reaction. He was watching me the way a child watches someone open a gift they've made for them.

I swallowed and added, "I appreciate the effort."

"Honestly, this has been nice. Being here with you. It's been a long time since I was able to do anything for you." His voice cracked and he looked down at the table in front of him again.

Was he crying?

Lord this was getting weird again.

"Okay," I clapped my hands together. Ready to be done with all of the nonsense and on to fixing my obviously mixed up brain signals. "Enough already. We need to figure out what mental health center we're going to go to tomorrow."

Zak's body deflated. His wings sagged behind his back. "You still think I'm not real."

"I don't know what else I'm supposed to think, Zak. The police could not see you. The 9-1-1 operator could not hear you. You are telling me you're an angel. Of course you're not real."

"I saved your cell phone from crashing against the wall," he offered.

"That would be an easy thing for me to imagine."

"What about the hole in your ceiling? The feathers all over the floor?"

I glanced up at the ceiling. "That could have fallen because it was put up incorrectly." I looked down at the floor. "The police already said they didn't see the feathers. They must be part of my illusion." I smiled, intensely proud of my ability to break his examples down into more sane explanations.

Zak pointed at the empty plate in front of me. "I made you something to eat."

Granted, him cooking in my kitchen, putting food down in front of me, and me eating it was an incredibly detailed illusion. But it was still an illusion, obviously.

I tapped my forefinger against my temple. "The human brain is extraordinary. All of this has been nothing more than a misfiring of synapsis and, to me, it seems absolutely real. It's fascinating when you think about it."

I sat back and crossed my arms in front of me. Satisfied that I would have this little break down conquered in no time flat and be back to my normal life.

Zak watched me steadily, looking pained at first, then discouraged, then troubled.

"Elsie, listen. I know this is a lot to take in and I'm sorry I've put you in this situation. Believe me, I'm sorry. But I'm your guardian angel and there's no amount of therapy or brain synapsis treatment, or whatever you can throw at it, that is going to get rid of me. Because I'm real."

I narrowed my eyes and gave him a piercing look.

"Prove it."

Six

Elsie

"You aren't religious," he stated.

"Not especially."

"You don't think you could try having just a little faith?"

"Not likely," I said, yawning. I was exhausted. "Why don't you keep thinking and I'll lay down for a while."

I went to the living room and curled up on my couch. I wasn't comfortable going to bed in my bedroom with a stranger in the house. Real or not.

The last thing I remember was him murmuring to himself as he paced slowly around the living room, a trail of molting feathers following him.

When I woke it was morning.

First I noticed there were no feathers on the carpet. Glad to see he could pick up after himself at least.

I stood and stretched and started toward the kitchen when I noticed the front door.

It was completely fixed. I ran my hand along the edge and

bent down to check out the deadbolt and the cracks in the wood that the officers had made when they kicked it in. Nothing. The wood and the broken lock and doorknob were all back to normal. As if none of that had ever happened.

Cautiously optimistic, I made my way to the kitchen. When I stepped around the corner everything was in pristine condition. There were no feathers anywhere to be seen. The ceiling fan was exactly where it had always been, whirring busily above the table. No rope discarded on the floor. No suicidal angel either.

"Thank God," I said, my knees wobbling as relief flooded through my body. I put my hand on the wall to steady myself.

For one moment I thought maybe I had dreamed everything, but I didn't believe that. No, I definitely had experienced a mental breakdown, but now it was over. I could research some good therapists, explain what had happened and get whatever treatment I needed to keep it from happening again.

"Thank God for what?" Zak's voice came from behind me.

I screamed and leaped into the air about five feet.

Whirling around I smacked his chest, pushing him away. I screamed again, this time out of frustration.

"You're still here!" I yelled.

He nodded. "Yes, I am."

I wanted to kick something. Break something. Cry.

"Why are you still here?" I demanded to know.

"I can't go anywhere, Elsie. I'm *your* guardian angel. Where you go, I go."

"I thought," I gestured to the cleaned up kitchen. "I thought you had disappeared. That everything was a dream or something. The door. The ceiling fan. Everything was normal." I was rambling, I know. I was so frustrated and upset.

"I fixed the door. And the ceiling fan," Zak said matter-of-factly.

"The door doesn't look like it was ever broken," I argued in a weak voice.

He almost smiled. "I know. I can make a cell phone float in

the air. You don't think I can fix some wood and metal on a door?"

"I don't know what to think," I answered, my earlier mood destroyed by his presence.

"Do you want some breakfast?" he asked with hope.

"No, I don't want any breakfast. I want you to go away, okay? That's all. Just go away."

The almost smile faded away and his face sank. He searched the kitchen as if he would find an answer there. There was none.

"I can't do that, unfortunately," he said.

I sighed and slumped into a kitchen chair.

"I think I worked it out though, while you were sleeping."

"Worked what out?" I closed my eyes, hoping against hope his voice would fade away and when I opened them again he would be gone.

"Well, when I tried to, you know, off myself, I think I messed up some time space spiritual veil thing. That's why you can see me now."

I opened my eyes. "Now? As opposed to you being here and I could not see you before?"

"Yes," he said. I stared at him. He explained, "I've always been around, but you couldn't see me before that happened."

"I don't know if I'm comfortable with that idea."

He shrugged. "You'll have to take your complaints to the Big Guy, because that's how it works."

"Can the Big Guy help us now? Put you back wherever you came from?"

Zak looked contrite. "He's not speaking to me right now. I don't know if he ever will again after what I did. I'm not sure he can."

I stared at him again. For a long time. Until I realized he must be out of ideas on the matter.

"So that's it? You're just going to live here in my house forever? Guarding me?"

"I guess so. It hasn't been that bad since last night, though. I mean, I was able to fix the door to keep you from getting robbed or assaulted. And I fixed the ceiling fan so you wouldn't fall or get electrocuted trying to fix it yourself. It's been a good twelve hours or so. Better than the past ten years."

I blinked at him. "Well, Zak, I'm glad you're enjoying yourself."

"You sure you're not hungry?" This time he did smile, just a teensy bit, the corners of his eyes crinkled ever so slightly.

"Any progress on proving that you're real?" I asked. I wasn't going to let him side step that issue.

His face fell again.

I felt like a jerk, but I couldn't allow him to lull me into a sense of normalcy so I wouldn't seek help. Couldn't let myself get charmed by the imaginary man in my life and forget that he doesn't actually exist.

"I'm sorry to hear that, actually. But so it goes. I'll be spending my Saturday calling around and getting referrals to therapists, thank you very much," I said with finality.

There was a knock on the door and the muffled voices of children calling, "Aunt Elsie, Aunt Elsie, wake up." Two voices to be exact. My niece and nephew.

"Oh no! That's my sister. I'm supposed to babysit Amelia and Abe today!"

Zak had folded himself into a kitchen chair and was staring gloomily into his lap. He looked up at me.

I hopped up from the chair and shouted in a whisper, "Hide!"

Confused, he reminded me, "Nobody else can see me."

"Oh, right." My panic subsided. "Can you stay out of the way then? I'll try to get rid of them."

He shrugged, drooping further down into the chair.

When I opened the door my sister, Brooke, was fishing through her purse for her key. Amelia, four years old, and Abe, six, rushed past her and hugged my legs.

"Hey, I forgot we were doing this," I started.

"Nope. You are not canceling on me," Brooke said. She

stopped short when she got a look at my rumpled appearance. "What happened to you?"

"What?" I straightened the shirt that I had slept in and ran my hand over my hair, which felt wildly out of control.

"Hi Aunt Elsie," Amelia smiled up at me. "What are we going to do today?"

"Yeah, Aunt Elsie, what?" Abe asked, not wanting to be left out.

"Hi munchkins," I said, ruffling the tops of their heads. I looked back at Brooke. "I'm having an issue today. We might have to reschedule."

"Oh no you don't," Brooke said, backing away instead of coming inside with her children. "Brady and I have had this reservation at the golf course for weeks. You can't take this away from us. From me." Her eyes followed her children as they ran inside my house and jumped onto the couch. "I need this, Elsie. I've been under a lot of pressure lately."

"I know, I know," I sympathized. Brooke worked hard at her communications job and at raising her two children. I had never minded watching them on occasion when she and her husband needed a short break. But this was different. "I'm having some problems with too much pressure myself," I added.

Brooke looked me up and down. "You do look a little ragged, sis. But you don't have to take them anywhere or anything. Just put on a movie and hang out here. They'll probably just fall asleep."

"Aunt Elsie, I'm thirsty," Amelia yelled from inside the house.

Brooke stuck her head around me and yelled back, "Get a drink of water. Have your brother help you." Looking back at me she squeezed my arm and smiled. "You could use a nap yourself maybe. We'll be four hours. Five tops." She let go of my arm and went down my front steps, turning and waving at me before getting into their family minivan.

Brady honked the horn and waved at me as they drove away. I waved back. Nothing I could do about it now. I suppose the kids could watch a movie while I looked up mental health resources in my area.

I closed the door and turned to see Amelia and Abe standing still and quiet in the hall just outside the kitchen door. Both of them staring in shock at something outside of my line of view.

Fear shot through my stomach. I walked toward them, carefully, as if approaching a wild animal.

"Kids...?"

"Aunt Elsie," Amelia said quietly.

"Yes?" I was halfway to them.

"Why is there a man in your kitchen?" she asked.

"Yeah," Abe added. "And why does he have wings?"

SEVEN

Elsie

Zak looked more scared than I was.

Both of us were more scared than the kids.

Amelia tugged on my shirt as I stared at Zak, who was standing in the corner of the kitchen with his wings pressing up against the wall like a giant chicken trapped in a coop.

"Aunt Elsie," Amelia asked in a loud whisper. "Is he your boyfriend?"

"No!" Zak and I both answered at once.

I shot him a look that said *don't talk to my niece, guy who used to be imaginary and now I have to deal with for real.*

"No, he's not my boyfriend," I said, slightly calmer, but with a finality I wanted everyone in the room to understand. "He's my...my friend. He's just a friend that's, uh, staying here...with me. Just friends."

"I think she's got the part that we're friends," Zak said.

"Zak, I need you to let me deal with my niece and nephew, please. I don't need your help," I snapped at him.

Zak stopped talking and crossed his arms in front of his chest.

"Hi, Zak. I'm Amelia," Amelia said.

Jeez she was a talkative little thing.

Zak gave her a finger wave from his crossed arms and smiled. It was the first expression I had seen on his face that seemed remotely nice. Not depressed or anxious or filled with regret. Just a genuine smile.

Then I remembered Brooke would kill me when she found out I let her kids hang out with some random friend of mine that she'd never met.

"Let's not worry about being introduced–"

"I'm Abe!" Abe said.

I sighed. So much for no introductions. "Do you know what I think?" I asked.

They all looked at me, including Zak.

"I think Zak is going to go home so you guys can hang out with me this morning." I used my most high pitched fun voice to really get them excited.

"We want Zak to stay," Amelia whined.

Zak stared at me, confused. "Home?"

"Okay, okay, hang on, we need to talk about something. The grownups need to talk." I put one hand on Amelia's head and one on Abe's and steered them out of the kitchen into the living room. "You guys find a movie you want to watch and I'll be right back."

"Can Zak watch a movie with us?" Abe asked.

"Be back in a minute!" I told them and exited the living room.

When I got back to the kitchen Zak was still standing in the corner. Still confused.

"How am I supposed to go home? This is home," he said.

"Keep your voice down," I whispered.

"Okay, okay," he whispered back.

"What is going on?" I asked him.

"What?"

"Why can they see you? And hear you?" I whispered angrily.

He looked in the direction of the living room and back to me. "I don't know."

My head was throbbing. Then spinning. Then throbbing again.

"But Elsie," Zak whispered, moving out of the corner of the kitchen and closer to me. "They *can* see me. Do you believe me now?"

"I don't know! I don't know," I covered my eyes with my hands. "I'm so confused."

"It's not that confusing, is it? I'm your guardian angel. I did something...wrong...that made you able to see me, but nobody else could. Except now your little niece and nephew can see me and we don't know why." He thought about what he had just said. "Okay, so maybe it's a little confusing."

"I need to sit down." I grabbed the nearest chair with trembling hands and sat in it.

"I wonder if it's because of the nearer to God thing," Zak said, more to himself than to me.

"Nearer to God?"

"Yeah, there's this saying that when people are nearer to God they can see us. Angels, that is. That would include people who are about to die or little ones, maybe?"

"Maybe? Don't you know the rules?"

He bowed his head, ashamed. "I don't. My brain's still a little fuzzy from yesterday. Plus, you were my first assignment and you see how that worked out."

"Great, I got a guardian angel intern?"

"Not exactly an intern. The only thing I can figure out is they thought you would be easy, you know, because of how you are."

"How I am?"

He sensed I didn't like where this was going. He kind of shifted back and forth on his feet, not wanting to answer, but I kept my eyes on him and he finally caved.

"How you're so *careful* about everything. *Everything.* You don't miss a brushing or a flossing, you weigh out your food, you keep everything so clean." He looked around, dismayed at my neat kitchen. "You don't cross streets unless you have the light at the crosswalk. You always use your turn signal. You go to all your yearly checkups and follow all the latest health advice. You have to do everything so perfect all the time."

"How is that bad? That's how you're supposed to live life." I argued. I had raised my voice and Zak looked at me in surprise. I continued in a whisper, "What, my guardian angel wanted to save me from a cavity?"

He sighed, a heavy sigh like he had failed once more. He looked down into his hands and his wings hung low on his back. "It's not that. You never want to go for hikes let alone climb mountains. Or swim or ski or roller skate or even Zumba. You don't fly or take trains. If you do go somewhere you drive, always at the speed limit or less. You don't dance or drink or talk to anybody you don't know. I'm no use to you. You were right, what you said before, you don't need my help."

I stared at him. I had so many reasons for the way I lived my life. I didn't need to explain them to Zak or anyone else.

Still, listing it out like that did make my existence sound sort of...incomplete. Lacking. Pathetic.

I started to say something snippy, but he looked as pathetic as I felt. Head hung low, angel wings drooping like I imagined angel wings were not supposed to droop. I couldn't bring myself to sting him with words.

I rubbed my eyes. I was tired. Sleeping on the sofa had not been comfortable. Plus I needed to entertain Amelia and Abe.

I sighed. "Do angels eat?"

Zak looked up, interested. He shrugged. "We can."

"Follow me." Entering the living room with Zak behind me I asked the kids, "Did you find a movie?"

"Yes, yes!" Amelia jumped up and down in one spot, so excited to see Zak joining their movie time.

"Finding Nemo!" Abe answered, clicking the button on the remote to bring the movie to full screen.

"All right, Finding Nemo it is. I'm going to fix us some lunch. Do you want chicken wraps or–"

"Pizza! We want pizza!" Amelia said, still jumping up and down.

I shared a look with Zak. "She always wants pizza."

Zak nodded. He knew that already.

I started to explain to her that pizza was not on the list of lunch choices. The fat content was far out of balance for what their growing bodies needed.

But I stopped myself before I opened my mouth.

Looking down into Amelia and Abe's hopeful faces, then at Zak whose near deadpan expression made me realize he was expecting me to do the same thing I always did, I changed my mind.

"That sounds great, guys. We'll have pizza!"

eight

Elsie

The pizza, I must admit, was awesome.

I hadn't eaten pizza since early college days. Before I learned how much fat was in cheese and how carbs worked.

Movie watching was also a hit. I think I was bumped up several notches on the favorite Aunt list. Even though I'm their only Aunt, I do like to keep my score high whenever possible.

Amelia and Abe loved Zak being with us and, because kids are especially bizarre, they weren't even bothered by his wings. Didn't give them a second thought once the pizza was delivered.

We watched the movie, good movie by the way, and nothing particularly weird went on. Besides the obvious.

After an elaborate charade of pretending Zak was going home, when he actually just went out the front door and then into the back yard to wait for Brooke to pick up the kids, we were almost home free as far as keeping the angel living in my house a secret.

"Knock, knock!" Brooke pushed open the front door and the kids raced to greet her.

"Aunt Elsie has a boyfriend!" Amelia spilled the beans immediately.

Brooke was stunned. "What?"

I tried to look innocent. "No I don't, he's just a friend."

"Who?" Brooke looked around as if Zak was hiding behind the couch instead of behind the house.

"His name's Zak," Abe informed her.

"He's really nice and he has wings!" Amelia added. So much for them forgetting about the wings.

"Wings? What are you talking about?" Brooke tried to look amused, but I could tell she was itching to ask me questions. Or give me a lecture.

I laughed. Wasn't gonna even address the comment about the wings. She would have to think it was her kids talking nonsense, which they have been known to do.

"I have a friend named Zak. He watched the movie with us," I explained calmly.

"And ate pizza with us," Abe added.

Now Brooke was really shocked. "You ate pizza?"

I laughed again. When there's one layer of crazy after another, you just have to pretend it's all a big joke.

"Come on, you guys, let's find your shoes." I said. When in doubt about my sister, act responsibly with her children and she'll calm down.

Brooke wasn't fooled. She walked from the living room to the kitchen with purpose, shoving her head into the kitchen really quick, like she might surprise a man hiding in there.

I wondered what she would have done if she found him in the kitchen the way I found him in the kitchen. Talk about a wild ride.

I was nearly 100% sure she would not be able to see Zak, even though her kids could. Still I was glad he was safe in the back yard and not hanging out in the kitchen where I would have to pretend that I didn't see him at all.

Brooke looked me over with her normal mild reproach. "I can't believe you let some guy hang around with my kids without telling me...or introducing me at least."

"He's fine, you would like him," I lied. Brooke would hate a failed angel. She was more precise than that.

"So, when do I get to meet this Zak?" she asked.

I shrugged. "I don't know. Never, probably. I told you we're not dating. It was a fluke that he was here."

"A fluke?" Brooke studied my face for cracks in my story.

"He's coming to my birthday party," Amelia announced. She had pulled her pink tennis shoes with velcro tabs onto her feet and was sitting on the floor carefully sticking the tabs together.

"What?" Brooke and I both asked.

Amelia nodded with certainty, still focusing on her velcro tabs. "I told him it's almost my birthday. He asked me if I was having a party. I said a roller skating party. And I asked him to come. And he said he would come." Done with her story and her velcro tabs, she looked up at us with shining brown eyes.

"Are you sure he's okay?" Brooke asked me in a whisper.

I nodded, still reeling at how I could have missed that entire conversation during Finding Nemo.

"He's not a pedophile or anything?" Brooke asked, her whisper fiercer, her lips tight.

"What?" I was insulted she would need to ask me that about my friends. "Why would you think that?"

"You never know, Elsie," Brooke gave me a knowing look.

All I could think was, no, Brooke, you don't know anything. You don't know about angels or about getting taken down by the police in your kitchen or how your whole life can get turned upside down in one insane moment when you think you're just coming home to an excellently clean house and instead...instead...

I took a deep, calming breath, and said, "I'm sure he's okay,

Brooke. But I don't know if he is actually planning on going to her party."

"Will you find out, please?" Brooke asked, her voice back to normal, but pinched with annoyance. "I will need to update the RSVP list."

"For a five year old's roller skating party?"

That made her leave in a huff.

When the coast was clear I opened the back door.

Zak sat in my lime green Adirondack patio chair. Eyes closed, his face to the sun, surrounded by birds.

Birds perched on his arms, his shoulders, his wings, and on top of his head. Birds flew around in circles above him. Birds flitted in and out of the space around him. Landing somewhere on him for a second or longer before hopping off and flying joyfully around him again.

Sunshine shimmered in his hair and his wings. Those huge, awkward, almost obnoxious wings, gleamed opalescent in the light, emitting a brightness all their own.

I stopped. Stunned by the beauty of him.

After a long moment, he opened the eye closest to me, squinting to see if I was there.

"Hey," he said. In a whirling rush of wind and feathers the birds were gone, leaving Zak in the sun. Alone.

"Hey," I stepped onto my small deck and sat down in my other Adirondack chair, the dark pink one.

"Did the kids go home?" He opened both eyes and sat up in the chair, his wings stretching wide as if he had just woke from a nap.

"Yeah," I nodded, thinking.

Zak waited, watching me. After several minutes when I didn't say anything, he asked, "What do we do now?"

I looked up. "Now, we figure out how we're going to fix this."

nine

Elsie

We spent the rest of the weekend, my weekend, I don't think angels count days, trying to figure out how to put the world back in order.

Not that I relished the idea of an invisible Zak following me around day and night ready to save me at a moment's notice. But that would be better than a *visible* Zak following me around day and night moping and sighing because I didn't need saving.

"I'm a naturally careful person," I explained again as I washed the apple I was about to eat with produce wash. "I was born cautious."

Zak watched me, frowning. "I don't think anybody's born like that," he jerked his chin at the produce wash then shuffled to the kitchen chair, sitting down with a heavy sigh.

"What do you want me to do? I'm a dietician. I know about pesticides. You want me to ingest poison so you can save me?"

"Isn't that an organic apple?" he asked.

I pressed my lips together. I didn't need a reason for every little thing I did. What I did need was a plan to get Zak back into the angel realm or wherever it was he came from.

"Let's go over this again," I said, sitting down opposite him.

Zak dropped his forehead on the table and groaned. "We've been over it a thousand times. I'm telling you I don't know how to fix what I did."

"Have you tried to remember how you might get in touch with someone else...up there?" I wiggled my fingers in the air over our heads and took a bite of my apple.

Zak raised his head to look at me. "Yes I've tried to remember and I don't remember. There's nothing there. It's blank. Dark. Empty. I don't know what happened or how to fix it."

"But you do remember watching over me before I could see you?"

"Yes."

"How long were you the one watching over me?"

"Almost ten years."

I took another bite of apple, chewed and swallowed. "And who was my guardian angel before you?"

He shook his head. "I don't know."

"You don't know or you don't remember?"

"What's the difference?"

"If you never knew, that's one thing. But if you did and you just can't remember then maybe you could remember again."

Zak's face sank. "I don't even know what that means."

"I don't either," I admitted. "I'm just trying to jog your memory."

He dropped his head back and stared miserably at the ceiling. "This is pointless."

"No, it's not." I refused to give up. It was one of my better qualities, I thought. "Do you remember anything about what you were supposed to do as my guardian angel? Like, were there instructions?"

Zak thought about it for a minute then raised his head suddenly. "I do remember something about that. I was supposed to watch over you, keep evil from touching you, yada yada yada. But also," He looked at me with a spark in his eyes. "There was something more specific. If you ever did something reckless. Something dangerous with no thought for your physical safety, I could step in." Confusion washed out the spark. "It had to do with something I was supposed to learn."

"Really?" I leaned forward. "What were you supposed to learn?"

I could almost hear his mind clicking as he tried to bring his memory to the surface. Then just as quickly as he thought of it, he lost it and let out a frustrated groan. "I don't know!"

Deflated, he sank back into the chair.

I, on the other hand, found encouragement in these nuggets of information.

"You said I was your first assignment, right?"

He grunted in agreement.

"So, from what you're saying now, I'm thinking that you were assigned to me specifically because you were supposed to learn something from me."

Nothing but a blank stare from him.

"Did you learn anything from me?" I took a big bite of my apple and chewed as he thought.

He shifted in his chair. "All I know is I waited and waited and waited...and *waited* for you to do anything remotely risky. And you never did."

I swallowed my bite of apple. "Never?"

"Not once."

"In ten years?"

"In ten years. Probably longer, would be my guess."

"Why would you say that?"

"Because a person doesn't just become that way overnight."

"And what way is that?"

Zak gave me a rueful look. "Afraid."

I snorted out a laugh. "I'm not afraid." I put my apple down on the table so I wouldn't choke on it while I laughed.

Zak's eyes followed the apple then flipped up to me. "You see?"

I did see. But he was being ridiculous.

"I am not afraid. I'm an adult and I don't talk, or laugh, with my mouth full of food."

"This is never going to work. You're never going to need me and I'm never going to remember how to get back. I screwed everything up again."

I set aside my irritation. "Again? What do you mean *again*?"

Zak paused, cocked his head and puzzled at his own words. The possibility of a memory returning hung in the air for several seconds. Then he slumped back into the chair.

"Sorry, I got nothing. I don't remember."

ten

Elsie

The next morning I got ready for work as quietly as possible. I wasn't sure if angels slept, but Zak had not stirred downstairs all night. If he was sleeping I didn't want to wake him up unnecessarily.

As I carefully opened the front door I heard a rustling. I turned and was startled to find him almost directly behind me.

"Going to work?" Zak asked.

"Yes." He was standing close. Really close. "What are you doing?" I asked.

"I'm going with you."

I laughed cynically. "No you're not!"

"I have to."

"You're not following me around at work all day," I argued, pressing on his chest so he would back up.

He took a few steps back, completely placid, and raised his arms slightly like he had no choice. "Where you go I go, Elsie."

"I refuse to let you come with me."

"You don't have a choice."

We stared at each other. Me trying to bully him with a nasty glare. Him waiting patiently for me to be done throwing a fit. Until I realized time was ticking by and I was going to be late if I didn't get moving.

"Fine," I said with a toss of my hair. "Come on."

I fumed as I drove. Zak, who had managed to fold his wings tightly together so he could sit in the passenger seat, watched the scenery go by.

Whenever I used my turn signal or slowed down with plenty of time to stop for a yellow light he would slide a morose look in my direction. I had to stop for a train and the look of misery on his face when I made an extra stop at the tracks after the train had gone by, just to be sure, was, I thought, over the top.

Finally, I had had enough of his presence. "This is stupid. I can't believe you have to come with me like a babysitter."

"I didn't make the rules," he answered gloomily.

"You could try to act a little more into it at least," I complained.

"Sorry, I just can't find any meaning in it anymore. I'm not a guardian angel. I'm nothing but a shadow."

I parked in the space I rented at the covered lot across the street from my work. Determined to not let Zak's presence get to me and to arrive to work on time, like I had for the past four years, I gathered my things and walked briskly to the sidewalk.

Zak lingered about ten feet behind, shuffling along like an oversized depressed vulture. It was so annoying.

I looked at my phone. I was going to be late. Kicking myself for getting behind schedule I glanced at the crosswalk, which was a half block away.

Zak had taken notice of my hesitation.

"What are you doing?" he asked.

"I'm going to be late, thanks to you," I snapped at him.

He came to my side and looked down at my feet. I was

standing on the edge of the curb. When he lifted his eyes to mine, they had a tiny questioning sparkle in them.

"Yeah, but, what are you doing?" he asked again.

I was so angry. I had worked hard for my perfect attendance and no tardies record. It was important to me. Important for my career. And here I was about to miss out on that because of my lughead guardian angel.

I stuck out my chin. "I'm crossing here. I don't have time to cross at the light."

At first my words didn't register with him. He just stared at me, stunned. When realization set in, the stunned stare turned into astonishment. Then pure elation.

"What!? Holy moly!" Zak turned around in a circle and ran his hand through his hair, trying to come to terms with my decision to violate pedestrian traffic laws. "I can't believe this! Seriously? You're serious!?"

"Shut up," I told him. "You're making a scene."

Zak laughed, a loud guffaw of laughter. He dismissed the few other pedestrians on the street with a wave of his hand. "Forget about them. I can't believe this. Holy moly. Holy moly. This is huge!" The joy on his face was transformative. He was positively glowing.

I, on the other hand, was not.

"My hands are sweaty," I said, shaking them nervously at my sides.

Zak jerked his attention to me. "Right, jeez, okay. Okay, I'm here. It's gonna be all right."

He bent over at the waist and held his arms out around my knees in a kind of air hug.

"What are you doing?" I asked.

He looked up at me, clearly excited. "I don't know. I'm offering my support."

"Are you going to carry me?"

"No, no, you're right." He stood up and stepped back. "I'll give you some room."

"Thank you."

My heart was beating fast. I positioned both of my feet so my toes were right on the edge of the curb, ready to step off. I tried to move, but it was like a wall of pressure was in front of me and I couldn't.

"I can't move," I said, looking at Zak. "Are you stopping me?"

He looked surprised. "No, what is it?"

"I don't know. I'm trying to take a step and I can't. I can't do it." This was unbelievable. I was terrified of stepping off of the curb.

Zak looked me in the eye. "You can do this, Elsie. It's okay." He moved closer without touching me, holding out his arms as if he had been assigned to guard me in basketball. "Here, I'll help you. I'm gonna go with you. It'll be fine."

I started to shake. "I'm scared."

He smiled. A warm, beautiful smile that filled his face and eyes completely. "Trust me. I've got your back."

"Trust you," I repeated. I took a deep breath trying to get it together.

Zak continued, calm and cool, "Just look both ways, you'll be fine."

"Look both ways, right. I almost forgot!" I let out a nervous laugh.

"That's okay. You didn't forget. You're fine. Here, look to the right," Zak instructed.

I looked to the right. The street was empty.

"See, nobody to the right. Good. Now the left."

I looked to the left.

"Your wing is in the way."

"Oh, sorry." He moved his wing back and I could see a pickup truck down the street heading in our direction.

"There's a pickup truck," I said, alarmed.

Zak had to squint to see it. "It's okay, Elsie. It's like, four blocks away. You're fine. You can make it."

"I can?" My heart was pounding so hard I thought it might

leap out of my mouth when I spoke.

"You can. It's only 30 feet, maybe 35, to the other side." He touched my elbow and I looked up at his steady gaze. "I'll be with you the whole way. I promise."

"Okay, you'll watch for the pickup?"

"If that pickup gets too close I'll send it to the moon."

I sucked in a deep breath and stepped off the curb. As I hurried across the street Zak kept his back to me and his arms stretched wide, circling around me like I was a quarterback with the ball and he was going to make sure I made it to the end zone.

He shouted out encouragement along the way. "This is great, Elsie! You're doing great. You're halfway there. Good job! The pickup turned. It's gone. Not even coming this way. You're safe. I've got you. Almost there! Keep going...keep going...YES!!"

Relief rushed through my veins when I stepped onto the curb. I had to catch my breath because I had been holding it while I crossed.

Zak leaped up and down, pumping his fists. His wings flapped with each jump, creating little bursts of wind. "Yes! Yes! We did it! *You* did it, Elsie!"

I was shaking, but I laughed at his celebration. Almost immediately, my laughter brought tears to my eyes.

Zak was looking back at the street as if it was a wide river or huge cavern we had just crossed. "That's great, you did great! I can't believe it!" He looked at me, smiling, and saw my tears. He rushed to me, worried. "You're okay, right? You're not hurt?"

"No, I'm not hurt," I said. "I'm just shaking."

He took hold of my shoulders. My shaking stopped the instant he touched me. He looked me up and down carefully, checking for injuries. Finding none, he held my eyes with his.

"That was amazing. I'm so proud of you," he said. There wasn't the slightest hint of sarcasm in his voice.

"Thank you," I answered.

He let go of my shoulders and clapped his hands together, rubbing them with anticipation. "All right, let's go to work!"

eleven

Elsie

Okay, so maybe I had a problem.

Maybe I hadn't been avoiding crossing streets outside of the crosswalks all this time because I was a grown adult who followed pedestrian rules. Maybe there was more to it than that.

The thing was, I didn't have a lot of time to worry about why crossing the street was such an epic challenge for me. I was walking into work at 8 o'clock on the nose. I had never arrived at my desk without at least five minutes to spare. Not once.

Usually I was at least 15 minutes early, sometimes as many as 30.

Not this day.

This day I slammed my purse, water bottle, and insulated lunch bag onto my desk just as the clock turned to 8:01am. I was out of breath, frazzled, and being followed by a rather excited guardian angel with the wingspan of an overgrown California condor.

"Aren't you pumped?" Zak asked.

I glared at him until his childlike smile dimmed.

Glancing around to make sure nobody would see me talking to thin air, and finding that my co-worker's desks were still empty – most of them strolled in 10 or 15 minutes after eight on the average – I placed both hands on my desk and leaned forward. Zak leaned away, wary of what I was about to do.

"You are not to speak to me while I am at work, do you understand?" I hissed at him. "You are not to ask me questions, not even rhetorical questions. You are not to get my attention, show me anything, or engage with me in any way. If anyone sees me talking to somebody who is not there, they will think I am crazy and I could lose my job. Do you understand?"

Zak nodded. "Yes, I understand." He glanced around at the still empty room. "Where do you want me to be?"

I waved at the corner of the room behind me and to the right. "There."

"No problem," he said. "And when does all of this officially start?"

"It starts now, Zak. Now! No questions. No talking. Nothing!" If I whispered any louder the friction in my throat would send me into a coughing fit.

"Okay, okay," he held up his hands in surrender and moved to his assigned corner. I could still see him in my peripheral vision when I turned my head, but that was the best place for him to stay out of the way. It would have to do.

I tried to settle into my routine by booting up my computer and checking my schedule. Zak stayed put, but in the silent office I could hear him breathing, which was a little distracting.

My co-worker, Beth, was the first person to arrive after me. Beth was the party planner of our office. Very talkative, engaging, a real positive thinker. I tried to avoid her when I could.

She hurried to my desk.

"Good morning, Elsie, how was your weekend?" Beth asked.

"Great, it was great. How was yours?"

"I'm glad you asked," Beth took in a deep breath. I

cringed. This could only mean she had a lot to share. "I was out with my friends, Marty and Melissa, I know them from college. Anyway, Marty wanted to show us this great place he went to at his last office get together. I guess every few weeks his whole office goes for happy hour somewhere really neat and this was one of the neatest places they had been in a while. Anyway, it's called The Dump and I think that's where we should go for our monthly office after hours thing? What do you think?"

"I'm sorry, did you say it was called The Dump?"

She laughed, which was to say her eyes squinted while she emitted a sort of twittering sound. "Yes, can you imagine? It's got to be great with that kind of name."

"Does it?" I was less than convinced.

"Anyway, I just wanted to tell you about it because you've never come to one of our after hours get togethers and I thought maybe if you knew where we were having it you might change your mind this time."

"You thought I might come because you were having it some-place called The Dump?" I wasn't sure how to feel about this, but I heard Zak snicker. It took everything in me not to turn around and shush him.

"No, silly, because of where The Dump is," Beth clarified.

Didn't help. I was still utterly confused by the entire conversation. "Why, where is it?"

"It's in LoDo! Won't that be fun? The whole downtown thing?" Beth said excitedly. She thought of something else and gasped, "We could share an Uber!"

There was his snickering again. I waved my hand discreetly at him behind my back and the snickering died down.

"Thanks for the invitation, Beth, but I don't think I can make it," I said.

"But I haven't told you when it is," Beth answered.

I stared at her, trying to think of what to say. Just then, my first appointment of the day arrived, Mrs. Mary Ann Clancy.

"Oh, look, Mrs. Clancy is here." I smiled, happy to have a reason to evade Beth's question.

Beth turned to look at Mrs. Clancy, a morbidly obese woman in her late 40's who had been sent to us by her doctor for help in losing weight. Mrs. Clancy was positioning herself in the chair at the far end of the row of chairs we had set up in our small waiting area. She had to sit on the end because her large bottom needed room to spread out.

Beth shook her head in dismay and leaned closer to me, speaking low, "She doesn't look an ounce smaller than when she first came in. They're going to have to do LAP-band or something on her."

Sure enough, Mrs. Clancy reported she had not weighed any less at her latest doctor appointment a few days before.

"Hmm, did you bring the food diaries I gave you?" I asked.

"I did! Let me see, where are they?" Mrs. Clancy searched through her faux-leather overstuffed purse, finally pulling out several slightly mangled food diaries.

Fighting the urge to grab her purse, dump its contents on my desk, and throw out all of the useless items and literal trash, I took the wrinkled food diaries with a smile and smoothed them out on my desk.

"Let's see," I looked carefully over the handwritten entries of every bite of food she had eaten, every glass of water she had drank, and every minute of exercise she had participated in. "It appears you did everything perfectly." I looked up at Mrs. Clancy's puffy face.

"Really? Perfectly?" Mrs. Clancy laughed. She was always laughing at something, this one sounded a little more nervous than her average laugh.

I tried to look kind, but concerned. "There is a problem, Mrs. Clancy."

"There is?"

"Three weeks of perfect calorie consumption and energy

expenditure in a woman your size should have resulted in a weight loss of approximately five pounds."

"It should?"

"And you say you didn't lose anything when you weighed at the doctor's office?"

"Actually, I gained three pounds." An unexpected giggle sputtered out of her mouth.

I heard a rustling behind me and almost turned to see who it was, but then I remembered Zak was back there watching. I ignored him and went on.

"I can only guess that perhaps you weren't completely truthful on your food diaries?" I asked.

Another giggle bubbled out of her mouth as she pointed at two words written in tiny letters posted on the second Tuesday under 'Snacks'. The words read *one doughnut*.

"Sorry, I didn't see that entry. So you had one doughnut?" She nodded. I sighed. "Mrs. Clancy, one doughnut in a three week time period would not make you gain three pounds."

"It wouldn't?" Mrs. Clancy's face sagged.

"You must fill these food diaries out truthfully or there's no reason to use them," I instructed.

All of the sudden I felt Zak's presence directly behind my chair and verified it with a quick glance to my side where I could see his giant wing invading my space. Why was he crowding me?

"Now tell me, how many doughnuts did you have?" I asked Mrs. Clancy.

She squeezed her eyes together and bowed her head. "A dozen."

"A dozen doughnuts? On that one Tuesday?"

She nodded. Not giggling anymore, she stared at her hands, which were clasped tightly together and held uncomfortably over her bulging stomach.

I scratched out the word *one* and wrote above it *twelve*. "And were there other days that you ate something you weren't supposed to and then did not write it down?"

She nodded silently, still staring at her hands.

I pulled open my top drawer to retrieve three new food diaries for her. "Now, you need to be sure to include everything you eat. It doesn't do you any good to–" I stopped talking because Mrs. Clancy had started to cry.

Huge tears slid down her cheeks and her hands, still clasped, moved up and down as her belly bounced with each sob.

"Mrs. Clancy, what is it?"

Between hiccuping sobs, she said, "I'm–never–going–to–lose–weight!"

I didn't know what to do. Beth and a few others were looking in our direction, wondering why Mrs. Clancy was making such odd noises.

Before I could stop him, Zak stepped around my desk and put his hand on Mrs. Clancy's shaking shoulder. He caught my eye as he did, his face full of sorrow. Almost immediately, her crying lessened.

Zak jerked his chin at the new food diaries I had gotten out for her.

"Now?" I mouthed at him.

He nodded, with an empathetic look at Mrs. Clancy.

I got it. I was to give her better instructions. Maybe soften my tone a little bit so she wouldn't get too upset.

I cleared my throat. "It's all right, Mrs. Clancy. You'll get the hang of this and then you will lose weight."

"You really think so?" she asked hopefully.

Inspired by Zak's kindness I added, "I do. And I'll be here to help you all the way."

Zak raised his eyebrows in mock surprise at my bedside manner.

"You're so sweet, Elsie," Mrs. Clancy said, taking the new food diaries. "I appreciate all of your help."

"I just want what's best for you. Start fresh with these and don't worry so much about being perfect. Just do your best and write down the truth and we will go from there."

With many thank you's and a lot of fresh giggling, Mrs. Clancy was on her way. Zak retreated to his corner of the office and sat on the floor, bending his knees in front of him.

Checking to make sure nobody was watching I turned my chair and whispered, "What was that about?"

He shrugged. "People just need to know someone is supporting them. You know, to get through the rough patches."

"I thought you were only here to support me," I teased.

Zak grinned. "I am a multi-faceted guardian angel." He wrinkled his forehead with a question. "I thought we weren't supposed to be talking?"

"Shush," I said, turning back to my desk.

Zak spoke up again behind me, "What about going to that party at The Dump?"

"Absolutely not," I answered.

twelve

Elsie

When we drove home after work, Zak's mood seemed improved. He wasn't as excited as he had been when I crossed the street that morning, but still he appeared to be in a decent headspace.

"Can I ask you something?" He spoke up as we pulled out of the parking garage.

"Sure."

"What is it about going to happy hour that you don't like?"

"The office after hour get together?"

"Yeah, happy hour. Any happy hour, really. I've never seen you go to one."

I would have thought my reasons were obvious, I mean, why do most people not like happy hour? But since he asked. "Crowded, noisy, drunk people, weirdos lurking outside...um, what else?" I tried to think of more. I had plenty of reasons, I knew that much.

"But what about the fun?"

"People don't have fun at happy hour," I scoffed.

He laughed, "Yes they do."

"Give me an example of something fun at happy hour," I demanded.

"You know, laughing with friends, getting a little tipsy, cheap happy hour food, dancing, good music, that kind of thing?"

I looked at him. He was being sincere.

"I'm not friends with people from my work, happy hour food is not healthy food, I don't dance, and I can listen to good music at my house. And I can get tipsy at home...if I wanted to."

He looked at me, surprised. "You don't dance?"

"Nope."

"Like, at all?"

I gave him a sideways glance. "Have you ever seen me dance?"

He thought about it then shook his head 'no'. Still curious, he asked, "Why not?"

I didn't know exactly how to answer that question and had to drive for a few minutes to think about it.

"Do you like music?" he asked, unable to wait for my response.

"Sure, I like music." I thought of a reason. "I've never really had many chances to dance."

Zak kind of laughed. "Everybody has chances to dance, don't they?"

I bristled at the question. "Maybe it just never came up."

He looked at me, clearly baffled. "Didn't you have dances in high school?"

I nodded. "I wasn't very popular. I was kind of skinny, a little too serious for everyone else." I shrugged, not bothered at all by my lack of a social life growing up. "Besides, nobody ever asked me..."

Eyebrows raised in surprise, he studied me as I carefully maneuvered the tricky intersection halfway between my work and my house.

"Your dad didn't teach you how to dance when you were little? Standing on his feet?" he asked.

That was a really specific question.

"I don't remember anything like that," I said. My hands gripped onto the steering wheel. "My parents died when I was nine. I don't remember either of them teaching me how to dance."

Zak sat silently in the passenger seat, contemplating my danceless life.

"Don't you know that already? I would think you would know something like that, being my guardian angel."

"I knew about your parents. I was wondering about before, when you were a little girl."

"Oh..." I kept my eyes straight ahead. I could feel Zak watching me. There was no more to say about the subject, so I told him, "Like I said, I don't remember."

Dinner was simple and fast. I was worn out from our long day at work together. I didn't know how I was going to keep this up. Having Zak around was exhausting. Knowing he was always nearby, always watching, it made me second guess myself about things I had always taken in stride.

"I think I'm gonna go to bed early," I yawned. "We can't give up on finding a way to fix this," I waved my hand back and forth between the two of us. "But I'm too tired to think about it right now."

"That's okay, Elsie," he said. "You get some rest. I'll think on it."

Bleary eyed, I paused. I had a question for him. "Do angels sleep?"

He smiled warmly, but I thought I caught a twinge of sadness in his eyes. "No, we don't need to sleep."

I did. I was asleep before my head hit the pillow. A deep sleep with no dreams whatsoever.

And I would have remained that way all night, waking rested and ready for my next day, if Zak hadn't woke me up in the wee hours of the morning.

"Elsie, Elsie," he whispered.

I moaned and rolled away from him.

He wouldn't give up and lightly shook my shoulder. "Elsie, wake up."

The circumstances of my life at that point were that I awoke to a full grown man with huge wings on his back crouching at the side of my bed, and I didn't even flinch.

"Zak? What are you doing? What time is it?" I asked, reaching for my cell phone.

"I don't know. It's early. But Elsie, guess what?"

Joy danced across his face and he was giving off a kind of glow so I could see him very well even in the dark.

"Guess what?" he asked, insisting I respond.

I collapsed back onto my comfortable pillow with an exasperated sigh. "What?"

"I think I figured out a way to contact the other side!"

thirteen

Zak

Hey, it's Zak.

I know, I know, this was supposed to be Elsie's story, but I wanted to check in for a minute and let you know what happened on my end of things. Because Elsie couldn't always see everything that I saw, which is probably good, really. Not sure she needed to see any of that. None of you do. Not yet anyway.

But I did want to give you a little information about what happened when I finally contacted the other side. My side.

As you may have picked up, I'd been having some problems in the guardian angel arena. Ever since Elsie and I kinda got stuck with each other, her seeing me and everything, I hadn't been in contact with anyone on my side. That was pretty unnerving for an angel. We're not all knowing and all powerful as you might expect. How was I supposed to fix things if I couldn't get proper instructions?

To be totally honest, my troubles started long before I woke up on top of Elsie in the middle of her kitchen floor with a rope around my neck. I had been struggling with my angelic purpose. Watching over Elsie wasn't what I thought it would be. And there was something else keeping me from being the best guardian angel I could be.

What was it, you ask? I couldn't have told you.

All I know is I had this problem before I suffered the major memory lapse with Elsie. Then I was in real trouble. I couldn't really remember any of the basics, not even how to get in touch with the Big Guy.

Then we were driving back from her job and something happened.

I remembered something about a dad dancing with his little girl. Her feet on his feet. That's why I asked Elsie about it. I thought it was her. But it wasn't.

I got to thinking. If it wasn't Elsie and her dad, who was it and where did that memory come from?

After she went to bed I got real quiet and sorta let that memory of the dad and his daughter float around in my head. After a while, the memory got real detailed. I could hear the music playing, feel the carpet underneath my feet, smell a meatloaf cooking in the kitchen .

Then all this rainbow light started quivering around the dad and the daughter and it got brighter and brighter until I couldn't see them anymore, it was just rainbow light all around me.

That's when I heard a voice.

"ZakZakiel."

It was a woman's voice. And that's when I remembered that the Big Guy was actually a Big Girl. Always had been.

"ZakZakiel," she said again, kind of impatient with me.

"Yes, I'm here," I answered. Then I had a rush of memories about talking to this rainbow light. So many memories coming all at once, it was like a waterfall of memories of me and this rainbow light, all of them were her trying to explain how to handle guardian angel problems. In layman's terms I think you might have called her my direct supervisor.

"You have disrupted the balance," she said.

"I'm sorry, I know I shouldn't have done that. That was a real misjudgment on my part. I messed it all up, I know," I tried to sound as remorseful as possible.

"The balance is not easily restored," she said.

I was crushed. I knew what I had done in Elsie's kitchen was going to be a problem, of course it was. I had committed a major infraction against God, against angels in general, and against myself.

"Yeah, yeah, I totally understand. It's just, I was hoping that maybe there was something I could do to put everything back the way it was. Before. You know, back in balance somehow?"

"There is."

"Oh, there is? Great! That's great, thank you. I'm really grateful."

Then there was just silence. Me and the rainbow light floating all around with only a white noise sound in the background.

Finally, I asked, "Um, so, how do I go about doing that?"

Loud and clear. Really loud. She said, "Make a positive difference in the life you have been entrusted. Life is not to be recklessly thrown away or abandoned. Then the balance may be restored."

"Okay, great! No problem. Make a positive difference in the life I've been entrusted." I was so excited to have some instruction that I didn't really digest what she had said. After mulling it over for a minute as the light shone and the white noise got louder and louder inside my head, I asked, "And how do I do that exactly?"

No answer. Nothing but glowing rainbow colors and me, wondering how I was going to make a positive difference in Elsie's life.

Then, poof, just like that, I was back in Elsie's house.

fourteen

Elsie

"A positive difference in my life?" I wanted to clarify that I had heard him correctly.

"That's what she said," Zak answered, a huge smile on his face.

He was standing at the side of my bed, hands on his hips, wings at the ready, as if he was a superhero about to take off and fly – and considering picking me up and taking me with him.

"But I already have a very good life," I sat up in bed, resenting being woken up, but also resenting the insinuation of the rainbow light lady that I needed someone else to make a positive difference in my existence.

"Do you?" Zak made a heavily sarcastic wince face.

"Yes, I do. I have a great job. I'm healthy. I have this nice house. I have a nice family..." I could have gone on and on, but I could tell none of it was getting through to Zak. He was gazing down on me with an annoying confidence in his eyes, as if he and he alone knew what was best for me. "What? What do you have in mind to make my life better?"

I shouldn't have asked. The question released a cascade of ideas out his angel brain.

"I've been thinking about it and I think what you don't have is fun. And I'm good at fun. I think I'm here to help you have more fun. Take risks, you know. Get out there and dance a little bit, push yourself, sail for distant horizons, all the things you don't do because you're too scared. That's what I'm here for in the flesh. Well, maybe not flesh, but you know what I mean. I'm supposed to stand by you and give you the courage to climb mountains."

I stared at him. This was a lot to take, especially in the middle of the night.

"Zak, I–"

"You don't have to worry about planning anything either. I can do all that. I think I may have some past experience with sports and outdoorsy stuff." He looked down at his lumberjack shirt. "Maybe that's why I've got this on instead of regular angel clothes."

What I had been about to say escaped my mind as a new question popped in. "What do regular angel clothes look like?"

He thought for a moment, but came up blank. "I'm not sure. But I bet they aren't all flying around in red and black plaid." He laughed at his own comment. If angels had adrenaline rushes, this was probably what they were like. I realized he was just all psyched up from speaking to his superior, the rainbow light lady.

"Look, I don't want to climb mountains or go sailing. We can talk about other options tomorrow. In the daylight. When I'm awake. I've got to get some sleep. I need to go shopping for Amelia's birthday present tomorrow after work."

He pointed at me. "Amelia's birthday party!"

"What about it?"

"We could roller skate. It's a roller skating party, isn't it?"

"I'm not even sure you should go."

"She invited me."

"She's four."

"She's turning five," he corrected me.

"She's five then."

"Still, the wish of a five year old means a lot where I come from."

I scowled at him. "You don't even remember where you come from."

"I remember that much. Besides, where you go–"

"I go. I know." I sighed, "It's late, Zak. Can you please take your happy dayglo self out of my room so I can go back to sleep?"

"Okay, okay, but will you think about roller skating at the party? It will be fun."

"Fine, I'll think about it, but I doubt it will be fun," I said, burying myself back under the covers as he backed out of the room, smiling happily.

It turns out that when you give an angel the tiniest bit of encouragement, they do not give up. Zak was relentless about the roller skating party the next day at work, after work when we went shopping for Amelia's present, and every minute of every day leading up to the party. I finally relented, agreeing to take one spin around the roller skating rink with him at my side to make sure I didn't crack my head open.

I wasn't looking forward to it, but it was the only way I could shut him up. And keep him from planning something more crazy, like a whitewater rafting trip or bungee jump, for me to experience.

When we walked into the roller skating rink I spied the party immediately. Brooke had dressed up a large corner table with pink and silver balloons, pink crepe paper and a huge silver foil spray table centerpiece.

Zak and I had gotten pretty good at talking in public discreetly over the past week. We could hold a decent conversation as long as I didn't look at him or raise my voice above a whisper. For the most part people just thought I was talking to myself, if they noticed at all.

"Do you really think she'll like it?" Zak asked.

He was referring to the gift he had helped me pick out. A pair of purple butterfly wings that she could hook over her shoulders. Zak had been particularly taken with the idea of giving her wings, go figure. As soon as we had arrived in the parking lot, however, he had started questioning the choice. I was forced to reassure him several times.

"Yes, I do," I reassured him again.

"She won't think I'm being pushy?"

"No, I'm sure she will love them."

Brooke waved at me as soon as she saw me. She was surrounded by children. Amelia and Abe split away from the group of kids and ran to greet Zak. I guess angel guy outranked favorite aunt on the list of exciting guests at a children's birthday party.

Before they got to us I reminded him, "Remember our cover story?"

"Yep, when the kids talk to me you can talk to me. And you'll tell the adults that you're playing make believe with them."

He barely finished talking when Amelia and Abe reached him. He stood as close to me as possible, trying to make it look to the casual observer that the kids were talking to me.

"Hey guys!" he said.

"Zak! You came!" Amelia was beside herself with excitement. Wearing a bright pink dress and silver leggings with a matching pink and silver bow in her dark hair, she was the picture perfect little girl.

"Happy birthday, Amelia," Zak said. His smile was genuine. I was pretty sure it was mandatory that angels like little kids.

"Come meet everybody." Abe grabbed Zak's hand and tugged him toward the group of children.

I realized too late that it was likely many, if not all, of the kids at Amelia's party would be able to see Zak in all of his angelic glory. I was going to have to stick by his side to make sure all of the parents simply thought I was playing along at having an imaginary friend. Lucky for us I only saw Brooke and Brady, their friends Laura and Christopher, and Aunt Millie, of course.

Aunt Millie was my father's sister. Mine and Brooke's only living relative. When my parents were killed in a car accident it was Aunt Millie who stepped in and raised us. More than an aunt, almost a mother, she was in her late 70's and doted on Amelia and Abe like any grandmother might do.

Abe pulled Zak to the group of kids. I followed.

Then Abe made a loud introduction, "Look, this is my Aunt Elsie's boyfriend, Zak!"

Though I cringed at Abe's use of the word 'boyfriend', I chose not to argue the point in front of a group of little children.

From the looks on all of the kid's faces they could definitely see Zak and his impressive white feathered wings. He got a little carried away with the attention and stretched them wide behind him so the rapt crowd got the full effect of their magnificence.

There was a collective gasp from the group of kids.

I shoved my elbow into Zak's ribs. "We're supposed to be low key, remember?" I said under my breath without looking at him. "So nobody thinks their kid has gone crazy?"

"Right, sorry," Zak folded his wings back down and smiled warmly at the children.

Brooke was glaring at me from the other side of the large table. I waved at her with Amelia's present.

"Okay, kiddos! *Zak*," I used my hands to mime around the edges of Zak's body so the parents knew that I knew the kids were speaking to a pretend person. "Zak and I are gonna help Amelia's mom with the cake now."

"What are you doing?" Brooke was in full annoyance mode when we reached her side of the table.

"What?" I handed her Amelia's present to put on the pile of presents next to the cake.

Brooke didn't answer, just increased her glare.

"Zak didn't come, obviously," I explained. "And Amelia seemed upset so I told her we could pretend he was here. Like an imaginary friend...kinda."

"Why are you so weird these days?" Brooke asked.

"I'm not weird."

"Zak did too come to my party," Amelia interrupted. She alone had followed Zak and I to where her mother was setting up the food. "He's right here!" Amelia pointed at Zak, who looked sheepishly at me.

"See, look what you've done," Brooke snapped at me.

I squatted down so I was eye level with Amelia and spoke quietly to her, "I have a secret to tell you about Zak."

Amelia leaned closer to me, but was still staring up at Zak. I motioned to him to squat down next to me, which he did.

I started again. "Zak's practicing being invisible today."

Amelia's eyes grew wide. She looked at him and he nodded gravely in agreement.

"So your mom and dad and all the other grown ups aren't going to be able to see him."

"But I'll be able to see him, right?" Amelia whispered back.

"Of course you can," Zak reassured her. "I would never be invisible to you."

Amelia smiled. "Okay."

"Good, now you have to go tell all the other kids so they know to act like they can't see Zak. We don't want to hurt their parent's feelings, do we?"

Amelia ran off to impart these new instructions to her friends and I was feeling pretty proud of myself for my scheming mind.

"You ready to skate?" Zak asked.

Bad Girls by Donna Summer had started playing and several excited skaters were already rolling around the rink to the rhythm of the song.

"Hang on, I'm gonna say hi to Aunt Millie," I told him, pretending that I wasn't stalling.

Aunt Millie sat on the carpeted wall bench that stretched all around the table and chair area of the roller rink. Zak followed me as I hurried over to her and leaned down, kissing her on her cool wrinkly cheek.

"Hi Aunt Millie, how are you?" I asked.

She grasped both of my hands and smiled up into my face. "I'm good, sweetie. How are you?"

"Good as always," I smiled back.

She glanced behind me, watching the activity of the rink, paused, then looked back up at me, a funny smile on her face. "I understand you brought an *imaginary* boyfriend to the party?"

"Yes," I laughed. "Amelia told you?"

"Oh, I saw the whole thing." She took one hand of mine in hers and patted the top. "Are you going to roller skate with the other young people?"

"Actually, yeah, I think I will this time," I said, nerves fluttering madly in my stomach.

Aunt Millie nodded her encouragement. "You go skating with that invisible boyfriend of yours and promise me you'll try to have a good time."

"Okay, I will," I answered.

Brady, who was wearing skates and carrying several pairs of children's skates, saw me by Aunt Millie. He raised up the children's skates as if offering to give me a pair. "You skating, Elsie?"

He meant it as a joke, of course. Brady had known me a long time. He and Brooke had been married nearly ten years. He knew I had never ventured out onto a roller rink.

The butterflies in my stomach rose up into my throat, because I had now made two promises to roller skate. One to Zak and one to Aunt Millie.

Zak looked at me with a twinkle in his eye. "You ready for this?"

I sighed and nodded. If I wanted Zak to go back to where he'd come from I had to keep up my end of the bargain. Butterflies or not.

I gave Brady a quick wave and a smile as I headed toward the skate rental counter, calling back, "I think I'm going to give it a whirl."

I thought Brady was going to topple over in shock.

fifteen

Elsie

When we finally hit the rink, Donna Summer's Bad Girls was over. In fact, several other songs had played while I made sure to get the correct fit on my rented roller skates.

Normally I'm a size eight, but the puke brown rental skates in size eight had felt much too big. Probably stretched out after years of wear. Yuck.

Thankful that I'd had the forethought to wear extra long socks so no part of the rented skates would touch my skin, I carefully laced up the seven and a half pair I got from the counter to replace the eights.

Zak had dropped into a nearby plastic chair waiting for me to get ready. His head hung back and he was staring at the ceiling, overcome with boredom.

"I'm ready," I announced when I had made sure the laces were evenly taunt and tied firmly at the top.

He didn't hear me. Three teenagers who were lacing up their

skates nearby did. They all turned to me when I spoke, shared a look with each other, then burst into a fit of giggles.

I waved my hand at Zak, but he was still staring at the ceiling. I couldn't call out his name, the teenagers were still within earshot. I looked down at the wheels on my feet. I was still in the carpeted area. I'd never roller skated before, how hard would it be to roll over the carpet to where Zak was sitting?

Harder than I thought, it turned out.

I pushed myself up off the chair. So far so good. I had stood up successfully. Taking note that I was significantly taller wearing roller skates than in my normal shoes, I wondered how much that height difference would make if I fell.

Zak was still gaping at the ceiling, not noticing my movements at all. Some guardian angel.

I pushed one foot forward a teensy bit and it rolled smoothly. My arms raised on each side to keep my balance. I inched the other foot forward so both of my toes were even.

Not bad. Not bad. I'd moved maybe two inches?

I heard snickering and turned my head to shoot a nasty look at those obnoxious teenagers, but I didn't get the chance. The move put me off balance and my right foot rolled out in front of me unintentionally. I tried to put all of my weight on my left leg to remain upright, but only succeeded in putting pressure on the skate so it started to roll backward. Quickly.

I threw my arms wider and higher like a panicked tight rope walker. I was about to do the splits in front of a group of sniggering teeny boppers.

I opened my mouth to scream what would be, hopefully not but most likely, a string of obscenities, when there was a rush of wind and feathers and a pair of strong hands on my waist, lifting me into a straight standing position again.

"Up you go," Zak said, holding me steady as my skates slipped forward and backward uncontrollably underneath me.

"Oh my God," I said.

He grinned. "Not quite."

I grabbed his upper arm to get my balance and was surprised at how firm and muscular and...*human* it felt. Zak didn't let go of my waist, which was good because my feet were sliding wildly back and forth. I couldn't get them under control.

"Steady, steady," Zak said.

"I'm trying to steady," I snapped at him.

Remembering the teenagers, I clamped my mouth shut and didn't speak, which forced me to breathe through my nose. With my breath coming faster and me trying to concentrate, I was snorting and grimacing like a cartoon bull.

"Here, I'll hold you up," Zak said, moving to my side and wrapping one arm firmly around my waist. He held me sideways up against his body so there was no weight on my skates at all.

Finally my feet were still. My legs dangled with the wheels of my skates barely skimming the carpet. I already felt like I had run a marathon.

"I don't think I can do this," I whispered.

"Sure you can, just put your arm around my waist and I'll hold you up."

I did as he said. The sensation of pushing my arm along his flannel shirted back and underneath the incredibly soft and warm feathers of his wings temporarily distracted me from anything roller skating related. For a moment all I could think about was what a strange situation I was in.

"There you go," Zak interrupted my thoughts. "Hold on to me. We're going to move, but I'll follow your lead. All you have to do is push one foot forward then the other and I'll make sure you don't fall."

Averting my eyes from him I whispered, "Don't you think this looks strange to everyone?"

Zak scanned the room. "Naw, nobody's looking."

As I pushed one foot forward then the other, I glanced back and saw that the three teenagers were most definitely looking. Staring in fact, with their mouths dropped open.

But I didn't have much time to worry about who else might

be wondering how my chaotic and abnormal movements were keeping me upright on roller skates, because we were already at the edge of the rink.

Every muscle in my body tightened as I gawked at the disco ball lighting that flew in random patterns across the shiny, extremely hard looking, roller rink floor.

"I can't, I can't," I squeaked, white knuckling the grip I had on Zak's waist.

"I've got you, Elsie. It's gonna be okay. I promise. Just take one step and I'll show you." Zak's voice was so calm, so kind.

"Do I have to keep my eyes open?" I whispered.

He chuckled. "No, I'll steer."

I closed my eyes, scrunching them together as hard as I could, then put my right foot out. With a sudden whoosh we were gliding, flying. Zak's arm stayed firm around my waist.

"Good, now put your left foot out," he instructed.

I did as I was told and the flying sensation continued. The wheels of my roller skates whirred along the surface of the floor, but I felt weightless. We were moving so fast there was a breeze on my face, the sound of feathers whipped through the air and, oddly, I thought I smelled funnel cake.

I opened my eyes, half expecting to be floating high above the other skaters. But, no, I was floating around the rink, the disco ball lights dancing around my feet as I pushed my right foot forward, then my left, then my right.

Zak made sure to move me the way a regular roller skater would be moving. In fact, it seemed like he was skating himself. I looked down at his feet and was surprised to see his boots were gone, replaced by sparkling white roller skates.

"Hey!" I said, looking up at him. "Where'd you get those?"

Just then a new song started. The bass intro for Play That Funky Music filled the air. Zak's eyes twinkled.

"This is a great song," he said, bending his wide shoulders forward and swaying his hips with the rhythm as we skated. "Come on, Elsie, here we go."

I did my best to follow his lead, giving up on trying to control the situation. Zak seemed to have things well in hand and I thought, why not? When would I ever be roller skating with an angel to classic funk again in my life? Most likely, never. May as well enjoy it.

So, with no more resistance from me, we skate danced around the rink until the song was over. Plus three more songs after.

sixteen

Elsie

Swift on the heels of our roller skating success, Zak wanted to do something else *fun*. Ruling out anything that required me to be belted in or sign a waiver left us with a singular upcoming event that he would not stop pestering me about.

Happy hour at The Dump.

In the interest of helping him fulfill his angelic assignment, I agreed to attend my monthly office happy hour, which made my co-worker, Beth, ecstatic.

"Oh my God, Elsie! This is exciting! You never go anywhere with us," Beth patted her hands together as she made tiny hops up and down in front of my desk.

"I think you may be disappointed with my presence," I warned her. "I'm not that much fun."

"Oh, but you are! You will be, at least, when you get into a more relaxed environment."

Knowing she was probably incorrect and carrying the additional pressure from Zak to enjoy the outing, I found myself parking my car in a dismal part of town after work the following Friday. I had spent twenty minutes driving around the area and found the only open parking meter within eight blocks. Happily, it was next to what appeared to be an abandoned warehouse.

"This looks just great." I peered through my windshield at the seedy street stretching between me and my final destination two blocks away, the illustriously named bar, The Dump.

Zak was unfazed. "You could have shared an Uber with Beth and the others."

I shot him a sarcastic look, "But where would you have sat if I did that?"

He grinned. "I've got tricks."

I rolled my eyes. Not enough tricks if you asked me.

The Dump's neon sign glowed bright blue and red in the late afternoon light. Several lamps lined the street, but weren't on yet because it wasn't quite dark enough. There were straggling pedestrians on the crumbling sidewalks, none of whom looked like employees leaving work for the day. Most of them were what I might call a little sketchy.

"Come on. You don't want to be late, do you?" Zak asked.

"I don't even want to be here."

"We don't have to go. There are other things we could do," Zak said.

I knew the kinds of things he was thinking about. He had listed them to me as possibilities on the way home from Amelia's birthday party. Horseback riding, water skiing, hang gliding, these were just some of his suggestions.

No, I was better off running the gauntlet from my car to The Dump and back.

"I'll go. I'm just not sure of the neighborhood, that's all," I said.

"That's why you have me." Zak grinned. "I see anyone get even a little bit too close to you and I will take them down."

Surprisingly, that did make me feel better. Though I doubted an angel would actually take anyone down.

"And what about my car? Is it safe to leave it parked here?"

Zak shrugged. "I don't know. I don't protect material objects."

Feeling less than reassured, I got out of my car and started down the sidewalk toward The Dump. Zak followed.

I wasn't even halfway down the block when a man walked past me going the opposite direction. He wasn't dressed in a suit or even in business casual attire, and he didn't seem especially friendly, but I managed to keep my panic at his proximity to me under control as he walked by.

A couple of seconds later I heard a thump and a muffled "Oof" behind me.

I turned around in time to see Zak slamming the guy to the ground right up against the building we were passing.

"What the...?" I was shocked.

Zak jumped off of the dazed and confused man and jogged back to me, smiling from ear-to-ear, his wings stretched wide and intimidating.

"How was that?" he asked, brushing debris off of his forearms and chest.

I had to remind myself to whisper. "What did you do to that man?"

Zak looked back at the guy who was getting on his feet. "I took him out."

"Was he about to grab me or something?"

Zak shot a suspicious glance at the man. "I don't know. Maybe. He got too close to you, I know that much."

Flustered at what he'd done and not wanting to face the stranger he had tackled, I decided to keep moving. I turned and started walking toward The Dump again.

Zak fell in step beside me. "Was that too much?"

"Maybe a little too much, yes," I said, keeping my voice low, but my sarcasm high.

More people were heading my way. Two men this time. They

were big guys and involved in some kind of lively conversation with each other.

My palms started sweating and I wasn't sure why. Either it was my normal anxiety when in the vicinity of strange men or I was worried Zak was going to pulverize them with his superior angel strength.

Right before they passed me, one on each side, they both stopped talking. Fear shot through my chest. Zak stepped behind me.

There was a thump. Then another.

I slowed down and turned to see what had happened. Both men were sitting on their rumps in the middle of the sidewalk, staring at each other, completely perplexed.

Whirling around to avoid eye contact with them, I quickened my pace. Only the intersection and another half block remained then I would be at The Dump.

"Was that better?" Zak asked when he caught up to me. "I didn't flatten them. Just kinda set them down on the ground."

I pushed the walk button at the crosswalk and glanced back at the two men who were standing now, looking at me with bewildered expressions. At least they weren't hurt.

Zak was waiting for an answer and I wanted to scold him, I really did, but instead I sort of snorted out a laugh.

Zak let out a laugh of his own. "So, that's okay? You feel safer?"

The Walk sign came on and I stepped into the street. Zak immediately jumped next to me, put his hand under my elbow, and scanned the intersection in all directions as I crossed.

I laughed again. "Maybe you're being a little overly enthusiastic, but I have to admit I do feel safer."

"Good, now you're ready for happy hour," Zak said as they approached the front door of The Dump.

I was there and I was safe, but I wasn't sure I could say I was actually ready for happy hour.

seventeen

Elsie

"I don't know what to think, Elsie. Something's the matter and you're not telling me what it is." Brooke sat across from me at my kitchen table, her face all scrunched up with worry.

Truth be told I was having a hard time focusing on our conversation. My head ached, my stomach was tender, and my mind was fuzzy. I was hungover and trying with everything I had to keep that fact hidden from my big sister.

"Elsie, are you even listening to me?"

"I'm listening." I was also wishing she would keep her voice down. "There's nothing going on."

"Are you kidding me? Look at you." Brooke motioned to my bed head hair and rumpled pajamas. "Look at this place." She flung her arm toward the kitchen sink where two used coffee mugs and two unwashed bowls sat on the counter.

I tried to look at the small mess of dirty dishes, but the light from the window over the sink pierced my eyeballs and I had to avert my gaze back to the table between us.

"You're worried that I didn't do the dishes?"

"Yes, and the way you look. You don't look well."

Brooke's keen powers of observation were correct. I did not feel well. But that was because I had drank too much at happy hour, had to get a ride home, and ended up sleeping next to my toilet. All things I had never done in my entire life. Not even in college.

Of course, I couldn't tell her that fact. My drunken night out would really push her over the edge.

"May I remind you that you came here without calling on a Saturday morning. Maybe I just haven't had time to clean up." I suggested. A reasonable excuse, I thought.

She narrowed her eyes at me. "It's more than that. You're not acting like yourself."

"How? Because I haven't gotten dressed yet?"

She nodded vehemently. "Yes! But other things too." She pointed at me. "You roller skated."

I raised my hands like I was being arrested. "You got me!"

"Stop it. I'm serious."

"I know you're serious, but I don't know what the big deal is."

"You don't roller skate, Elsie. Even Aunt Millie noticed."

"Aunt Millie told me to roller skate, Brooke. What did she say about it to you?"

"She noticed that you were skating well and said maybe your invisible boyfriend was good for you."

I leveled my gaze at Brooke. "That doesn't sound like she's worried at all."

"She's not, but I am! And what about the whole invisible boyfriend thing? What is happening with this Zak person? He is a real person, isn't he?"

Zak, who had been leaning against the doorframe of the entry to the kitchen since Brooke arrived, raised his eyebrows at the mention of his name.

I ignored him. "First of all, yes, Zak is real, but he isn't my boyfriend. The kids keep calling him my boyfriend, but they're wrong." Zak shifted his stance in the doorway. I kept my eyes trained on Brooke, who was still looking at me skeptically. "Second, I told you I was just pretending he was there for Amelia's sake, so she wouldn't be disappointed that the real Zak didn't come to her birthday party." I wasn't sure my confusing explanation was helping convince my sister of anything.

Brooke scowled at me. "It's not normal for an adult to play make believe," she argued.

"I was playing with the kids, Brooke. It's not a big deal." I wished my head didn't hurt so bad or I would have gotten up and started slamming the four dirty dishes around in the sink to wash them.

Brooke sighed. "I don't want to fight. I'm worried about you."

I didn't want to fight either. And, in all honesty, I was slightly worried about myself. For reasons I could not go into with Brooke, obviously.

I was stuck with a guardian angel following me around and I wasn't sure his influence was totally positive. I mean, I had a hangover for heaven's sake. That didn't seem like something an angel should be encouraging.

My turn to sigh. I looked at my worried older sister who had left her children with her husband on a Saturday morning to come over and check on me. Ever since our parents were killed in a car accident when we were kids, Brooke had always watched over me. It was probably a hard habit to break.

"Do you want some coffee?" I asked. "I do."

Brooke nodded and I set about making a pot, moving slowly to keep the pain in my head at a minimum. Zak watched from his position in the doorway. He had been beyond supportive all night, pouring me into an Uber after we left The Dump, making me coffee when we got home, and holding my hair back when I finally got sick.

I glanced at him as I pulled two clean mugs out of the

cupboard, thinking it was strange that I couldn't offer him a cup. Not that angels needed to eat or drink, but he did appear to enjoy partaking of those human functions when we were alone.

Zak caught my eye and ticked his head to the right, which I guessed meant he was going to wait somewhere else while I talked to Brooke. I barely nodded my understanding. We had gotten pretty good at covert communication when others were around. By the time I started spooning ground coffee into the filter he was gone.

"So what is going on with Zak? Is there any romantic interest there?" Brooke asked.

Surprisingly, I hesitated before I could form my answer. This was evidence enough for my sister.

"You're into him, aren't you?" Brooke's eyes shone at the idea.

"No, I'm not," I answered as firmly as I could.

But in my mind I kept seeing Zak at happy hour laughing at the office jokes, feeling his arm around me as we roller skated, hearing his voice as he comforted me when I was sick from drinking so much. If I ignored the fact that he was invisible to practically everyone but me, that he had bizarre supernatural powers, and that he wasn't, in fact, human, Zak was kind of cute, nice, and fun to be around.

"Don't be ridiculous," I said, more to myself than to Brooke. I poured us both a cup of coffee and sat back down. "Trust me, he's not my type."

Brooke took a sip and put her cup down. "Is there anyone else these days who is your type?"

"Not really," I answered with an unexpected pang of regret.

"Well, maybe you're just not into the idea of getting married and having kids yet."

"Maybe."

"You never have been into weddings."

"Why would you say that?"

"Remember how you freaked out at mine?" Brooke chuckled at the memory as she enjoyed another sip of coffee.

I did remember. I was a senior in high school when Brooke married Brady, and I had, as she so aptly described, *freaked out* when they were getting ready to make their exit as a married couple.

"It wasn't the wedding that freaked me out," I corrected her. "It was the balloon."

"The hot air balloon?"

"Yes, the hot air balloon."

Brooke had wanted to do something different at the end of their wedding reception. She wasn't satisfied with waving as she was swept away in a standard limousine or even a horse drawn carriage. Nope, she and Brady had been lifted into the air in a tiny little basket. I had more than slightly panicked at the sight.

"I thought it was symbolic, you know? Brady and I floating up into the clouds after the reception."

"It was unnecessarily dangerous."

"The balloon was tethered, Elsie. We weren't going to float away or anything. It made for some good pictures."

"Well, there's that at least," I said, more than a little sarcastically.

"See what I mean? You're not the hot air balloon type. Which is fine. But it kind of freaks me out when you do things like roller skating. It's not normal for you."

"I know." I understood. It wasn't normal for me. "But you don't have to worry about me, okay?"

Brooke watched me carefully for a few moments, then said, "I love you no matter what. And I want you to be happy."

"Thank you, I love you too," I managed to say before I started tearing up.

I did love Brooke and my family. And she was right to be concerned about me. I was concerned about me. I had always been pretty sure of who I was and what I was doing, but things had changed since Zak appeared. I had changed.

If I wasn't the Elsie who was up and perfectly dressed early on a Saturday morning, or the Elsie who would never consider doing something like roller skating or getting drunk at happy hour, or the Elsie who was fine being alone...who was I?

eighteen

Elsie

After Brooke went home I called for a ride to take me to my car, which I had left parked near The Dump. I didn't ask Brooke for a ride because, seriously, having to explain to her why I left it downtown overnight would have been too much. There were no scrapes or dents, not even a parking ticket. I counted myself lucky.

By Sunday I had recuperated from my Friday night out, but I still wasn't ready to engage in any more Zak planned activities. I told him I needed some down time before attempting any more adventures. He responded by falling into a funk over everything that had gone wrong.

"I'm sorry The Dump didn't work out so good," he said, looking sheepish as he watched me in the kitchen.

"It wasn't the place. I was actually surprised at how nice The Dump was on the inside." I popped a sheet of cookies into the oven. Healthy chocolate chip, my favorite.

"Was it the company?" he asked glumly.

"No, everybody was fine. I didn't think I would have a good time with the people I work with, but I did."

"Was it me?"

Surprised at the way he said it, I turned to him. "It wasn't you. You were...fun. As fun as an invisible angel could be I guess."

He smirked and stared at his feet.

"I'm not convinced happy hour is as fun as you think it is, that's all." I told him. He seemed pretty let down that I wasn't thrilled about going again.

"Yeah, I wasn't expecting you to drink as much as you did, that's for sure," he admitted.

I stared at him. "You were the one telling me to have a good time."

"I also told you that Long Island Iced Teas were not the best idea."

That was true, he had tried to warn me off of those. "But they were so tasty. Although, thinking about them now kinda makes me want to ralph."

He smiled, starting to come out of his mood. "And you didn't dance. I'm telling you, if you want to have fun you need to dance more."

"There was nobody to dance with."

"What about, what's his name, that Felix guy? He would have danced with you."

I laughed at the idea. "Felix is probably almost 50."

"That doesn't mean he can't dance."

"That may be true, but he didn't ask me so we'll never know. Nobody asked, in case you don't recall."

"Would you have said yes if they did?"

I laughed again, fairly certain I would never attend another happy hour for the rest of my life so his was a moot point. "That's one more thing we'll never know."

Zak cocked his head and gave me a sly smile. "Would you dance with me? If I asked?"

I started to laugh again until I saw his expression. His eyes twinkled and that sly smile stayed on his lips. Almost like he was flirting.

Nerves fluttered through my body and I started wiping the counter top with a nearby dish towel. "Here?"

"Yes, here."

"Don't be silly. There's no music or anything."

The muted sound of brass instruments playing the beginning of Frankie Valli's *Can't Take My Eyes Off Of You* rose in my kitchen. I turned to face Zak, shocked. He raised his eyebrows in mock surprise at the sound of the music.

"I'm asking," he reached out his hands.

Talk about panic.

I wrung the dishtowel nervously. "I don't know how, Zak."

"I'll show you."

My heart was pounding and I didn't know why. There was nothing frightening happening. It was just my guardian angel dressed like a lumberjack asking me to dance around my kitchen to the sound of a classic 1960's love song magically playing. No biggie.

I placed the dish towel on the counter and put my hands in his as Frankie Valli's voice started to croon, *You're just too good to be true...*

Zak pulled me close, but not too close. He placed my left hand on his shoulder so he could move his hand to my waist. His shoulder was strong and warm. His wing feathers tickled my fingertips.

"Follow me," he instructed and stepped to one side then the other. I followed, propelled by the pressure of his hand on my waist guiding me. "Good, you're doing great!"

He sounded surprised.

I know I was surprised.

The music grew louder, leading into the chorus. Zak turned us in a circle and when Frankie's voice belted out *I love you baby*, Zak pushed me away from him, only holding onto one of my hands, and twirled me around several times until I was dizzy. When he pulled me back I was laughing.

"Hey, look at us! We're dancing!" Zak said, grabbing my waist again and turning us around the kitchen, shocking me when he managed to sing along with the lyrics and also keep his wings from bumping into anything.

He continued to sing to me as we danced, alternately making me laugh and making me blush, but never making me want to stop.

Suddenly, we were interrupted by a loud beeping sound.

"My cookies!" I pulled out of his arms and hurried to the oven.

As I grabbed my oven mitt and took the cookies out, the song ended. Part of me was relieved and part of me was sorry, but I didn't tell Zak about either feeling.

I turned to him, holding the cookie sheet in between us. "Want a cookie?" Then I remembered they were fresh out of the oven. "Oh, wait, they should probably cool off first."

"That's not a problem. I love chocolate chip cookies." Zak picked one up, broke it in two, and popped one half of it into his mouth, smiling as he chewed.

One micro-second later his smile turned into a grimace.

Alarmed, I said, "I told you they were too hot."

He grabbed the trash can from under the sink and spit the uneaten cookie into it.

"It's not that." He grabbed an empty glass and filled it with water.

I watched him rinse and spit into the sink then rinse and spit again before filling up the glass one last time and drinking it all without taking a breath. Finally he placed the glass on the counter and looked at me like he had been tricked.

"I thought those were chocolate chip cookies."

"They're healthy chocolate chip cookies." I picked one up and inspected its gooey goodness. "My own recipe."

"What's in them?" Zak's distaste for the cookies was so intense it was comical.

I couldn't suppress my smile. "I use carob instead of chocolate. It's high in fiber, lower in fat and sugar, and it's caffeine free."

"Ick," Zak complained. His face was still twisted with disgust. "Lower in joy, too. That is a joy-free cookie."

"Does that mean you don't want another one?" I teased.

"No, thank you. Those are all yours."

"Don't mind if I do," I said with a chuckle. Never a dull moment in my new weird life.

nineteen

Elsie

Monday morning at work, Beth couldn't wait to grab me as soon as she arrived. "Elsie, you're not going to believe–"

"Everyone, everyone," Mr. Jangmore, our boss, interrupted, stepping out of his corner office and calling for our attention.

Beth closed her mouth, but looked like she was about to burst from the built up pressure of not being allowed to speak. "You'll see!" she squeaked.

I followed her and my other co-workers to where Mr. Jangmore stood with a well dressed super hottie, apparently waiting to be introduced.

"Isn't he gorgeous?" Beth stage whispered at me, the sound of her voice easily reaching Mr. Jangmore and the hottie.

I tried to act like Beth wasn't whispering to me by glancing behind me as if to catch a glimpse of her conversation partner. Zak was lingering a few feet back, watching the commotion. He grinned, knowing I was embarrassed.

"Okay, everyone, settle down, settle down," Mr. Jangmore said.

He always spoke to us like we were a group of kindergarteners on a field trip. Looking around at Beth and the others, he had a point.

"I want you all to meet my nephew, Keith. He's joining our marketing and communications office as chief coordinator."

Murmurs all around. Beth sighed audibly. I, for one, kept my cool, mostly because I knew very little about the marketing and communications department. Keith's dark good looks and fashionable suit were kind of distracting, however. I tried to maintain my professional face. I didn't want anyone to guess I thought he was over the top attractive.

"Why don't you say a few words of greeting, Keith?" Mr. Jangmore told his nephew.

Keith cleared his throat. Adorable. When he scanned our group of about thirty employees, his eyes landed on mine and stayed there. I felt a little flippity-flop in my stomach when he started speaking. He had a deep, masculine voice.

"I'm excited to be here and I hope you won't hold my family origins against me," Keith said.

Appreciative chuckles rose from the crowd. Self deprecating. Nice. I smiled. Keith Jangmore smiled back at me.

"Other than that I'm just really looking forward to getting to know each of you and being part of the team," Keith finished.

Everyone clapped. None so enthusiastically as Beth.

She latched onto me as I was returning to my desk. "I told you," she whispered again.

"You told me what, exactly?" I spoke quietly, but not in a whisper, then immediately regretted asking.

"That you weren't going to believe how fine the new guy was."

Yep, I regretted getting involved in this conversation. As nonchalantly as possible, I said, "He's okay."

"Okay!?" Beth fanned herself with her hand. She giggled and shoved me playfully. "And he was checking you out for sure."

I blushed uncontrollably, which was aggravating. "Okay, for one, I don't think this is an appropriate work conversation. For two, no he wasn't." And for three, which I did not share with Beth, holy moly he was definitely checking me out!

I was able to abandon Beth before I got back to my desk by making a quick stop at the ladies room. Luckily she didn't follow me inside.

Zak, on the other hand, did.

"What are you doing in here?" I whispered hotly at him. Great, now I was the weird whisperer.

"Was that guy a creep or what?" Zak asked.

"Zak, get out of here. I told you that you couldn't come with me into bathrooms."

"There's nobody else in here."

I shot a look at the four stalls, all with closed doors. "How do you know?"

"I just know."

I glared at him. "I would like to use the bathroom without you hovering nearby."

He tilted his head and paused, giving me a look. "It's nothing I haven't seen before."

I gasped. "No, don't tell me that! Gross!"

"It's not a big deal."

"It is a big deal. Oh my God, Zak." I recoiled from him, scrunching my face up in disgust.

"Don't worry about it. Sometimes, in the name of safety, we have to...intrude a little bit on your privacy. It's kinda like special angel-client privilege."

I shut my eyes, but the creepy crawlies shimmied across my skin anyway. Repulsed and exasperated, I asked, "Why are you in here?"

"I thought you could talk in here, since we're alone."

Opening my eyes I leveled a burning look at him, but

managed to stay calm. "What is it you wanted to talk to me about?

Zak jerked his head toward the door. "That new guy. He was pretty creepy, looking you up and down like that. Don't you think?"

I narrowed my eyes at him. "Do you know what's creepy? You following me into the ladies room."

Zak crossed his arms in front of his chest and made a snorting sound.

I pressed my hand to my forehead. This was insane. The minute I thought I could handle this whole 'Zak goes everywhere with me' thing, something happened and I knew that I was going to go crazy if I didn't get him back into the Netherworld or wherever he came from.

Just to get him out of my hair, I answered, "I don't think the new guy's creepy. I thought he was cute, actually. But that's not what I need you to be worried about. We need to come up with more ideas that I can do that will satisfy your weird angel rules so you can go home. Okay? Why don't you worry about that instead?"

Zak wasn't satisfied. He turned his head and looked down at the floor next to him, avoiding eye contact.

To top off everything I really did need to use the bathroom. I clamped my mouth shut and pointed fiercely at the door. "Wait for me outside, please."

He shook his head and turned, his wings twitching with frustration as he left.

After work we had both calmed down quite a bit. I allowed Zak to give me directions to my next life lesson, which he had come up with after our bathroom conversation.

"You don't think I should know where we're going in advance?" I asked as I turned the car right on the street he indicated.

"No, because you'll have too much time to think about it."

I didn't like it, but he was probably right. I had told him to come up with an idea, and I did want the whole situation to be over with, so I went along.

After one more right and two lefts he had me pull over and park next to Brumley Park, one of the biggest parks in the city. I turned off the engine.

"This is it? The park?" I was surprised. It didn't seem that intimidating.

He grinned at me. "I figured you weren't ready for bungee jumping yet."

"You're hilarious," I told him before getting out of the car and joining him on the grass. The sun was bright and it was still nice and warm outside. I stretched my arms out to the side, enjoying the fresh air. "This isn't that bad. What do we do, walk around?" I glanced at the street where I had parked my car. "Do you think I should cross the street or something like that?"

"No, I have something else in mind. This way." Zak swept his arm toward the concrete path that went all around the edge of the park.

As we walked along the path I thought about what he had said, nerves rising in my stomach. "Do you really think I'm going to have to bungee jump to get you back into the angel realm?

He laughed. "I don't think so." He gave me a side eye look. "But I'll let you know if I get any instructions about it."

Terrific. I decided to try and focus on being as calm as possible as we walked around the park. Enjoy myself. Be full of fun.

It wasn't terrible. The pathway was a little uneven in places, probably a fall risk at times. There were a lot of kids running free, riding little bikes and skateboards dangerously close to the walking pedestrians.

Also a lot of dogs. Some of them appeared pretty mellow, but occasionally there was a giant beast of a dog that could easily rip away from its owner and attack if it so desired. Then there were some feisty little dogs whose owners allowed to roam without leashes. A clear violation of the park rules.

Still, I thought I was doing pretty well not freaking out about it all. I wasn't much of a park person, but I was handling it. Maybe Zak's encouragement really was helping me enjoy life more.

"I think this is nice. I feel like I'm doing really well on this challenge," I said happily. I liked calling them 'challenges'. It felt a little like I was on a reality TV show instead of living out this bizarre situation in my actual life.

Zak looked down at me as we walked, studying my face with a bemused smile. "You are doing well, but we're not there yet."

"We're not? Where are we going?"

Zak pointed further down the path and suddenly all of the pedestrians kind of magically parted, stepping to either side so I could see.

A hot dog cart.

twenty

Elsie

The hot dog turned out not to be the most terrible food I had ever eaten. After working through my initial concerns by pacing back and forth several yards away from the hot dog stand while mumbling to Zak about the endless number of reasons I definitely wasn't going to eat a hot dog, I ended up buying one.

Actually, I had to buy three, because Zak wanted two. And since he couldn't order for himself I was stuck at the hygienically questionable stand adding condiments to two of the hots dogs while Zak told me what he wanted.

"Aren't you going to put anything on yours?" he asked.

I shook my head 'no'. The extremely sweaty and hairy hotdog vendor was standing within earshot.

"Nothing? Not even mustard?"

After dipping condiments out of little cups which had been used by countless members of the public, including those who didn't wash their hands properly, and piling mustard, relish, onions, tomatoes, pickled garlic and olives on top of Zak's hot dogs, I couldn't stomach the idea of anything else on mine. I couldn't stomach the idea of ingesting the hot dog itself.

Zak frowned. "You gotta at least have mustard."

"Fine," I muttered, ignoring the odd look the hairy vendor gave me. I put a shot of mustard on my hot dog and carried all three of them to a secluded area on the grass under a big tree.

I watched Zak devour his first hot dog with a churning stomach. "Do you know what's in these things?"

"Sure, but that's not the point." He lifted his second hot dog up so I could look at it more closely. "The point is that millions upon millions of people eat hot dogs and nothing bad happens."

"I beg to differ. Heart disease happens to people. Processed meat is terrible for your heart, your cholesterol, your weight."

"You really think one hot dog is going to cause all of that in you?"

"No, of course not. But if you let one thing slide who knows what else might start to slide? And then you're on a big, out of control, sliding mess of disease and death."

Zak closed his eyes briefly and took a deep breath, releasing it slowly. "How long has it been since you ate a hot dog?"

"Probably since I was a kid. Like twelve or something like that?"

"I don't think eating one now will turn into a sliding mess of disease and death."

I eyed the hot dog. "Unless I choke."

Zak's face brightened. "That's what you've got me for."

I couldn't argue with that logic and I did want to do everything I could to help Zak get back to being an invisible guardian angel rather than one staring at me while I pondered eating a hot dog. So I took a bite and, like I said, it wasn't the most terrible experience I had ever had. A little rubbery maybe, but not awful.

I chewed and swallowed.

"They're good, don't you think?" Zak asked cheerfully, taking a bite of his second.

I shrugged, not wanting to admit that I might be able to enjoy eating a hot dog. "I'll survive."

We ate in silence for a while. Both of us enjoying the pleasant weather. I took careful bites of my hot dog, hating it less and less each time.

Out of nowhere, Zak asked, "Have you ever wondered what made you so..." he searched for the word. "Wary?"

The question was a little out of left field, but I was surprised to find it didn't make me immediately defensive. Zak's words sank down into the center of my heart and I knew the answer right away. I didn't, however, know the exact words to explain.

I let my eyes wander thoughtfully around the park. Runners, dog walkers, elderly couples, and parents pushing strollers moved purposefully along the pathway. Other people relaxed in the grass. A group of college age kids played frisbee. Several families with young children were scattered across the park, spending time with each other.

A flock of birds flew as one from a grove of trees nearer the street and landed in the tree we were sitting under. They chirped and hopped from limb to limb until most of them were sitting on branches hanging just above Zak and I. Zak didn't seem to notice, he was busy taking large bites of his overloaded hot dog and waiting to hear my answer.

Finally, I decided that I didn't need the exact correct language to explain what I knew in my heart. If I couldn't confide in my guardian angel, who else could I confide in?

"It was my parent's accident. The car accident that killed them," I said, speaking quickly. "I was only nine and I remember not understanding what was going on right away. Then, when I did understand that they were gone, that they weren't coming back, I didn't cry or freak out like Brooke. Not at first."

Zak nodded, quietly chewing and listening. The birds above us stopped chirping.

"I didn't cry for them because I was afraid. I was afraid for me." My throat and eyes got hot. I kept talking even though I was in danger of crying. "I remember thinking that if my Mom and Dad could die, then so could I. And I was filled with fear." I choked on the last word and clamped my mouth shut, holding back tears. A shiver went through me as the memory came on full force and I became that terrified little girl again.

Zak held very still. His face softened.

Two big fat tears escaped my eyes and rolled down my cheeks.

Zak reached over and took my half eaten hot dog out of my hands, placing it on his leg where his hot dog was also balancing. Then he took hold of my hand, which was trembling and cold. I could feel just how cold next to his glowing warmth.

He didn't say anything. Neither did I. I couldn't speak because my face was crumpled up trying to keep from crying...and failing. My heart ached too hard to form words.

When I looked back on this moment later, I wondered what the other people in the park thought as they watched a lonely woman ugly cry over two half-eaten hot dogs underneath a silent flock of sympathetic birds.

twenty-one

Elsie

The next happy hour outing for my office came around faster than I thought possible. Because of my hangover from the previous time I was prepared to give Beth a hard no when she asked me to go.

"Guess who's coming to happy hour?" Beth bounced excitedly on the balls of her feet. "Oh, you're never going to guess. I'll tell you. Keith, it's Keith!"

I stopped right in the middle of my eye roll. "Keith? The new guy?"

Beth nodded emphatically. "You're coming again, aren't you?"

"Well, um…" I glanced behind me at Zak who was leaning on the wall behind my desk. I cleared my throat. "I wasn't going to, but–"

"Oh, you have to Elsie. Come on. It'll be fun! And with Keith there it'll be even more fun," Beth giggled as she spoke.

Zak refrained from commenting and also from making any

gestures indicating what he thought I should do. I don't know why I felt the need to consult him on everything I did anyway. I was my own person after all. Besides, giving happy hour another shot would probably help him get his wings, or whatever we were trying to do.

"Yeah, I think I'll come," I answered.

Beth kind of flipped out that I agreed to go, but her excitement didn't stop me. The next night Zak and I attended my second happy hour and, frankly, I had expected Zak to be more upbeat about it.

"Why are you so gloomy?" I asked him as we approached the bar. Thankfully this happy hour was being held in a more suburban area at a Mexican place called Jose Oshea's. No scary warehouse buildings or nervous walk to the entry.

"I'm not gloomy," he said, gloomily.

"Isn't this what I'm supposed to be doing? Putting myself out there and experiencing life?"

"Yeah, I guess."

"You guess?"

Zak glanced up at the faux stucco walls of the building we were about to enter. "You already did one of these. I don't think you need to do it again. I have a whole list of new things."

"I'll do those, too. Don't worry. Believe it or not I actually wanted to come tonight."

"I can see that." He glanced quickly down at my outfit then back up at my face.

I had gone to more pains than usual to wear something a little light and fun instead of my normal well tailored, buttoned up look. I looked down at my clothes self-consciously. I had chosen a flowing white dress with a dainty flower print that Aunt Millie had bought me on an afternoon shopping trip. I had only worn it once before, to brunch with her.

I frowned. "I kinda thought this was pretty. You don't think so?"

Zak gave me a close lipped smile. "It's fine. You ready to go in?"

Once inside with my coworkers I forgot about Zak, or tried to at least. Besides Beth, there was Link and Wendy from accounting, Felix was there ready to party again, Kara and Tiara who were fellow dietitians, and, just like Beth had said, the boss' nephew, Keith Jangmore.

"Hi," Keith greeted me as soon as I arrived. He stuck out his hand. "We haven't met formally. I'm Keith, what's your name?"

"Elsie," I said, taking his hand, appreciating its warm strength.

"It's great to meet you, Elsie." Keith smiled and my knees buckled the tiniest bit.

He was even more handsome up close. Dark skin and hair, deep brown eyes, a close cut beard that accentuated his chiseled features. He smelled good too. Some kind of fancy cologne, probably, but it worked on him.

"What are you drinking?" he asked.

Beth answered for me with a giggle, "Long Island Iced Tea."

"No, no not that," I corrected her, automatically glancing back to see Zak's reaction. He wasn't right there like usual, but with a quick searching look I found his wings, and him, moping at the end of the bar behind us. Put out by his bad mood, I turned back to beautiful Keith and smiled. "I'll take a glass of wine."

Keith smacked his hand on the table as if committing my order to memory. "Perfect. Red or white?"

"White, please," I smiled again. He certainly did bring out the smiles in me.

"I'll be right back," Keith said, stepping away toward the bar.

As soon as he disappeared into the crowd, Beth grabbed my arm. "He has been asking if you were coming for the past half hour, Elsie. You're so lucky, he's totally–"

There was a heavy thump and "oof" sound behind us. I whirled around to see Keith sitting dumbfounded on the floor and Zak standing over him.

"Zak!" I called out without thinking.

Beth gave me an odd look. "That's Keith."

"Right, of course, Keith."

We hurried to Keith's side. He was a bit stunned though he didn't look physically hurt. Beth and I helped him up and got him seated at a stool at our table. Beth got him a glass of water and as soon as I knew he wasn't damaged, I grabbed my purse and excused myself.

Zak had gone back to the end of the bar and that's where I approached him. Steaming mad.

"Follow me," I said through my teeth.

Dutifully, he walked behind me straight to the bathroom. I pushed the door open so hard it slammed against the wall. Zak paused in the doorway.

"Elsie, I don't think we should–"

"Oh, now you don't want to do this? You were perfectly happy doing it the other day at my job!"

Zak lowered his head, but kept his eyes on mine. "You're mad."

"I'm mad!? Why would I be mad!?" I threw my hands up in the air. "All you did was take out my boss' nephew for absolutely no reason in the middle of a bar! Why would I be upset about that?"

Zak shifted from one foot to the other, his wings sagging behind him. Still, he didn't answer.

"Why would you do that, Zak?"

His jaw clenched several times as he stared fiercely at the floor, searching for an explanation. When he looked up at me his eyes burned with intensity. He tore his gaze away from mine and scrubbed the back of his neck. His wings shook with agitation.

For an instant I was afraid. Uncertain what kind of power Zak could actually unleash. What kind of damage he could do. But when he looked back at me, his eyes were quieter, apologetic even.

I tried to be logical. "I don't understand why you would do that to Keith. I like him. I might even want to go out with him. I would think it would be a good thing if I went on a date or two. Put myself out there and get over some of my issues."

"Not with that guy," he said with stubborn finality.

Before I had a chance to explain to him that it wasn't any of his business who I went out with, a toilet in one of the bathroom stalls flushed.

My eyes flew open. Someone was in the bathroom? I looked at Zak in surprise.

He jerked his head in a defiant nod. "I tried to tell you when you came in here."

The stall opened and a woman stepped out. She attempted to smile empathetically, but was obviously embarrassed and a little frightened to be caught in the bathroom with a lunatic.

Thinking quickly, I tried to laugh the situation off and offer a plausible explanation. I tapped my ear and said, "Bluetooth."

The woman nodded in understanding and moved to the sink to wash her hands.

That's when my purse started ringing, because that's where my cell was tucked away. The woman caught my eye in the mirror, giving me a strange look.

I didn't try to explain any further. I hurried out of the bathroom, pushing past Zak as I left in a rush.

twenty-two

Zak

Hi, Zak again.

Maybe you've caught on already that there was something kinda funny going on with me. Not me exactly. Mostly, all of my problems at that point had to do with Elsie.

Not the anger management problem. She's always kinda had a temper as long as I've known her. Definitely could be a little feisty sometimes...and stubborn. You know, just because she wanted things the way she wanted them. That wasn't the problem I was having. I never minded an opinionated woman.

No, my problem wasn't with how Elsie was acting. It was more of a problem with how I was reacting to her.

After the first few days went by when she could see me and we were working together to get me back to the angel realm, I started noticing how whenever she got upset, I got upset too.

I know, I know, that's the kind of behavior you might expect from a guardian angel, but there was something different about it with Elsie.

When she would get really sad, I wouldn't just feel sorry for her and want to help her. I would feel just as sad.

When she got scared, I didn't just want to protect her. All I could think of was protecting her and I didn't care who I hurt in the process. It was like I couldn't think straight anymore. I would just zero in on whatever the threat was and take it out.

And I figured that kind of attitude wasn't really what guardian angels were supposed to do. I know I didn't remember everything about being a guardian angel, but I was pretty sure we weren't supposed to mindlessly destroy everyone near our assigned client.

My reactions to Elsie's emotions just didn't feel right. Something was different. Something was wrong.

I didn't know what, though. That was the problem. I still didn't have all of my memory back and something major had changed with me.

So I decided to go to my angel supervisor and ask her opinion. Late on the night I took out Keith at happy hour, after Elsie went to sleep, I got myself relaxed and focused on the same little girl dancing with her father memory until the rainbow light showed up again.

"ZakZakiel." The rainbow voice moved around me through the light. Much more powerfully than the last time I had spoken to her.

"Hi, yes, it's me."

There was a long pause and I wasn't sure if she was waiting for me to talk or what.

Finally, she said, "You are troubled, ZakZakiel."

"Yes, yes I am. I'm, uh, having some trouble with Elsie."

Another pause. Rainbow light. White noise.

Then, suddenly, "What is your trouble?"

The volume and suddenness of her question startled me. "Whoa, okay, um, well I think I'm having some sort of feelings."

"Feelings?"

"Yes...I mean I know that it's normal to have feelings, I guess, even though I'm an angel? I'm not sure how that's supposed to work, actually. But these feelings are *a lot*. They're big, much bigger feelings than I think is normal."

There was another pause as my angel supervisor pondered my predicament. This was good. She would know what to do. I was glad I had decided to come to her with my questions. I waited patiently until she spoke again.

"Your feelings are good, ZakZakiel. It means the process is working for you."

"The process?"

"Yes, the process of making a positive difference in the life you have been entrusted. The life you recklessly threw away."

What? That last part was new.

"I'm sorry, what was that?"

"The process is working. When it is complete the balance will be restored."

"Wait, what are you talking about? The process is working on me? Not on Elsie?"

Silence again. I was afraid she wasn't going to answer and just plop me back into Elsie's house without any further explanation.

"Indeed. Your balance was disrupted. It is your balance that must be restored."

"My balance!?" I was so confused. "I'm Elsie's guardian angel. She's the one I'm supposed to be helping."

"Remember the dancing girl. Remember..."

And just like in a weird movie, her voice trailed off and blended into the white noise. I was left alone in the rainbow light for a few moments, shocked and confused by what she had said.

How had my balance been disrupted? I was supposed to be making a positive difference in my life, not Elsie's? I didn't understand.

No more answers came from rainbow woman. The light around me started to spin and before I could call out to ask her to clarify, I was dropped back into the middle of Elsie's kitchen.

This time I wasn't excited to have made contact with my

supervisor. I was more baffled than ever. And I was done. Really, really done with all of the cryptic nonsense.

twenty-three

Elsie

When I got up and went to the kitchen for some coffee the next morning I found Zak staring into space. He did not look good. In fact I thought, a little ironically, he looked like hell.

"What's the matter with you?" I asked.

He jumped like I'd startled him then looked around, coming out of a daze. "Is it morning?" He croaked before sinking back into his own thoughts.

My eyes slid to the bright sunshine streaming in through the kitchen window then back to Zak. I went about making a pot of coffee. Maybe angels didn't need food like humans, but Zak seemed to appreciate eating....and he looked like he could use some coffee.

It came to me that perhaps he was struggling because I'd gotten so mad at him the night before at happy hour. As I spooned ground coffee into the machine I tried to make him feel better.

"Look, I'm sorry I yelled at you. Although I still think what you did to Keith was..." I stopped talking, because I had turned around and seen Zak's face.

His eyes were vacant. They looked right through me. He seemed...hollowed out. Carefully, I approached the table and sat down opposite him.

"Zak...Zak!" I waved my hand in front of his face.

His head jerked back. Totally aware of my presence for the first time since I entered the room, Zak's eyes focused on mine, but they were still distant.

"Hi," he said.

"So, what's going on? You're all weird or hypnotized or something."

More of Zak returned to the present, thankfully. His eyebrows puckered. "Hypnotized?"

"I'm not sure if you've been hypnotized, but you're spaced out. You've been staring into nothing since I walked in the room."

Zak turned to the doorway as if expecting to see me come in. He ran his hand over his face in an attempt to wake up before looking back at me. "I've been thinking."

"Oh? Okay, what have you been thinking about?"

He shifted in his chair, eyeing me a little uncomfortably. "I contacted my...supervisor last night after you went to bed."

"The rainbow lady?"

He nodded. "She told me something...something I wasn't expecting."

The coffee machine beeped and I went to pour us some. "And? What did she tell you?"

"She told me it wasn't you I was supposed to fix."

I stopped mid-pour and looked at him. "What?"

Confusion filled Zak's eyes. He shook it off and held his palm out toward me to keep me from going off the deep end. "She told me what to do, though, so it will be fine. Don't worry."

"So I've been going through all of these little *assignments* for no reason?"

"No, not at all. At least, I don't think so."

Incredulous, I said, "That doesn't sound terribly reassuring, Zak."

"I know." He dropped his head into his hands and his wings slumped.

I opened my mouth to say something critical, but closed it instead. On one hand it was a relief to know that I wasn't solely responsible for getting Zak back to where he belonged. And, even though I wasn't going to tell him this, I had sort of ended up enjoying myself as I tried new and dangerous things. Maybe the whole situation had turned out all right for me.

I finished pouring two cups of coffee and brought them to the table. I sat in the chair next to Zak and put his mug in front of him. He didn't look up. Hesitantly, careful not to bump his wings, I put my hand on his shoulder and patted it.

He opened his fingers and looked at me with one eye. "Do you hate me?"

"No! Don't be ridiculous. How could I hate my guardian angel?"

His posture relaxed a little and he dropped his hands to his lap. He really looked terrible. Had he been that worried that I would actually hate him? Was I that big of a jerk that he thought me capable of being completely unsympathetic?

I kept patting his shoulder, struck again at how human he felt whenever I touched him. If he didn't have huge wings sticking out of his back there was no way I could tell he was an angel.

"Why don't you start from the beginning and tell me what the rainbow lady said?"

He explained the whole conversation they'd had during his little psychedelic trip to angel land. A sudden lightness overcame me, a giddiness at being off the hook and free of a great burden.

Unfortunately, my good mood was dampened by Zak's uncertainty. He was obviously upset and I sympathized with him. Plus we were still faced with the same problem of him being stuck in my world.

"Were you able to remember anything else about the dancing girl?" I asked helpfully, I hoped.

"No, I've been thinking about it all night. Trying to visualize anything else, you know? But I can't remember any more."

I rubbed his shoulder and a little down his back. He was tense. I thought. I mean, were angle back muscles always so hard? I didn't know.

"Maybe you're thinking too much about it. Maybe it's the kind of thing that needs to come out when you're more...relaxed," I suggested.

Zak turned and locked eyes with me. I was suddenly acutely aware of how close we were sitting and of my hand wandering up and down his back, kneading his muscles, feeling the way he was formed.

"Do you have any suggestions on how to relax? he asked, his voice gravelly from distress.

His dark hair was tousled and falling over his brow. His eyes were more green than normal and seemed like they were capable of peering deep inside my thoughts.

"Um," I stilled my hand on his back. I pulled it slowly away, putting it into my lap for safe keeping. "Not off the top of my head. Maybe, um..." I couldn't think straight, his eyes were still penetrating my mind. Without any warning, I laughed. A quick, high pitched sound that did not suit the occasion. I covered my mouth to stop it. "Sorry, I just had a thought."

One side of his mouth lifted in a teasing smile. "What's your thought?"

"That at least I'm not going to have to go bungee jumping."

He shook his head and chuckled.

My cell phone rang, pulling us out of the moment. It was not anybody I knew, but the same area code as mine, so I answered it.

"Hello?"

"Hi, Elsie? This is Keith," the deep, masculine voice on the phone said.

"Keith?"

"Yes, Keith Jangmore from work."

"Oh, right. Right," I gave Zak a sideways glance, knowing we were sitting so close and he could probably hear every word. "Hi, how can I help you?"

"Yeah, well, I know it's unusual for me to be calling you on your personal number. But I have a...a personal question for you."

"You do?" A small fluttery sensation started in my stomach.

"Yes, I was wondering if you would like to go out with me? On a date."

     # twenty-four

Elsie

I hadn't been on a date for a good long while, so I was a little nervous. I also had never been on a date while lugging along a six-foot plus invisible man with wings, but I was willing to give it a go.

Keith was cute. So cute. And he had an excellent job at a reputable company, this I knew for a fact. He hadn't overreacted when he "fell down" at happy hour, so I figured he wasn't prone to emotional outbursts. All of these were pros in my book.

Zak's book, apparently, had different priorities. He had been quite vocal about his dislike of Keith, but hadn't provided me with any concrete reasons not to go out with the man.

"I wish you wouldn't look at me like that just because I'm going on a date," I told him while I put on my shoes and checked my hair and makeup. Keith was going to arrive any time.

"Like what?" He was practically pouting.

I let out a heavy sigh. Zak had a wide variety of emotions for a supernatural being, in my opinion. But I wasn't going to let him get to me. I was already nervous enough, but excited too. And I had started to enjoy the way being excited made me feel energized.

"Just promise me you won't knock him over or anything rude like that," I said.

He gave me a small nod and shuffled his feet back and forth. "Fine."

When Keith arrived I got so caught up in the moment that I forgot all about Zak moping nearby. My insides were vibrating and I was a little out of breath.

"Good evening, Elsie, you look beautiful," Keith said, looking quite beautiful himself. All white teeth and well tailored clothes. "Are you ready to go?"

"Of course, thank you," I responded and took the arm that he offered.

After he opened the passenger door of his slick grey Mercedes for me and made sure I was settled before closing it and going to the driver's side, I saw Zak standing on the sidewalk watching. I suddenly wondered how he would ride along. As if in answer to my question, he stepped up to the back door of the car and vanished in a burst of rainbow sparkles before reappearing sitting squarely in the middle of the back seat, his wings taking up all of the room on either side of him.

I gasped. He'd never done that before. I wanted to ask him if he had always known how to do that or if his memory was coming back to him, but Keith opened the driver's side door.

"Sorry I'm a rush," Keith said as he slid into the driver's seat next to me. "But I don't want to be late."

Keith insisted on keeping our destination a surprise during the drive and I managed to ignore the giant angel man squished in the back seat. As far as first dates go, I thought it was pretty good so far.

It wasn't until we drove further and further out of the city and even beyond the suburbs that I began to wonder.

"You can't tell me anything about where we're going?" I

asked, a little apprehensive before I remembered my guardian angel was literally sitting behind us.

Keith smiled his winning smile and gave me a wink. "I can tell you we are just about there."

'There' turned out to be a wide open field just outside of a large suburban area. While I didn't see any buildings nearby where we might be dining, what I did see sent the vibrations I had been feeling inside my body absolutely wild.

Several SUVs and a pickup truck were parked along the edge of the field. Their occupants were all gathered in the center of the field around a large basket big enough to fit adult people. Attached to that basket and stretched out across the field was what appeared to be a deflated hot air balloon.

"Oh my God," I said.

Taking my reaction as a good thing, Keith gave me a shining smile. "Surprise!"

I didn't look back at Zak, but I heard him chuckle.

Keith took me to meet the balloon pilot, a swarthy looking man named Petrov. He had a Russian accent, which for some reason added another layer of fear onto the several layers that had already encircled my internal organs. I knew I wasn't being rational anymore.

"Hello, young people," Petrov greeted us warmly. "We'll be ready to go in a little while. As soon as Natalya is ready." He smiled at me like we shared a secret. "Natalya is the name of the balloon."

As the small crew of people blew air into Natalya with huge fans and blasted the flame thrower attached to the top of the basket to heat up the air and make the giant balloon lift off of the ground, I tried not to faint.

"Have you ever been in a hot air balloon?" Keith asked, obviously not about to faint.

I shook my head 'no', unable to form words.

Zak had rainbow sparkled his way out of the car and joined us near the basket as we waited for our ride. When Keith turned to

Petrov to ask a few questions, Zak leaned down and spoke into my ear.

"You okay?"

I nodded, swallowing hard. I was determined to have fun on this date. Besides I had already done lots of scary things with Zak including jaywalking, roller skating...eating a hot dog.

Zak squinted at me. "You sure you don't want me to take him out?"

I shook my head 'no' and swallowed again. I wished they would fill the stupid thing up already so we could get on with it.

As Natalya grew huge and buoyant, several of the crew members were assigned to stand around the outside of the basket and lean their body weight on it to keep the hot air balloon from floating away.

Keith looked at me, wiggling his eyebrows up and down. "It's almost time."

I managed a weak smile and gave him a thumbs up.

"Are you almost ready, love birds?" Petrov asked jovially. Without waiting for an answer he turned to another man nearby who was not acting as a human weight on the basket. "Boris, do you have the champagne?"

"I do, Captain," Boris answered, raising a green champagne bottle and four glasses.

Petrov swept his arm in a grand gesture toward Natalya. "Then it is time to board. We will toast in the air!"

Petrov and Boris got into the basket first, followed by me then Keith. Zak squeezed in last and it was a tight fit even with his wings pulled tight together and raised up as high as he could get them. On top of that, all four sides of the basket were packed with the crew who were leaning all of their weight on the edges and smiling at us. It was far from romantic, even putting aside the waves of anxiety that were shuddering through my body.

Petrov reached up and grabbed the flame thrower and I watched in dread as he pulled the handle forcing loud, long blasts of flame into the yawning mouth of Natalya. A red balloon with one wide white stripe and one wide blue stripe circling her middle, she might have been beautiful to watch...from the ground.

"Weight off!" Petrov shouted.

Every single crew member stepped back and away from the basket and we rose instantly into the air. I didn't have any more time to worry about what was going to happen. It was happening. My panic rose as quickly as Natalya.

"Wow, what a rush!" Keith said happily, slipping his arm around my waist as we were suddenly looking down at the tops of the trees that surrounded the field. He squeezed me into his side, which wasn't the thrill for me I think he was expecting.

Zak scanned the area with casual interest then, to get out of the way of Petrov and Boris, he hopped up so he was sitting on the edge of the basket next to me.

My stomach leaped into my throat and my eyes shot open wide. I remembered just in time not to call out his name. Instead, I made a squeaking noise and gripped the edge of the basket until my knuckles were white.

I was shaking like a leaf and was pretty sure I had turned green around the gills. Between the blasting of the flame to keep Natalya's air hot enough to stay afloat and Keith carrying on a boisterous conversation with Petrov and Boris, nobody noticed my reaction to the flight.

Nobody except Zak.

He watched me steadily from his perch on the side of the basket next to me. But he didn't make any effort to step in and help. I guessed that meant I wasn't in any danger. At least not at that point.

I wanted to tell him that I would feel a lot more comfortable if he would get off of the side of the basket. Seeing him there put a wobble in my knees. But of course, I couldn't speak at all. And he might have had a hard time reading my expression. Pure terror doesn't always look like what you expect it to look like on some-one's face.

"It's time for the love bird toast!" Petrov announced.

"That's us," Keith said to me.

Was it? I wasn't feeling very love bird-ish.

Boris handed the four champagne glasses to Petrov to hold, two in each hand. I wondered who was steering Natalya while this little ritual was taking place, but again, I was too queasy with fear to say anything. Holding the champagne bottle between his knees, Boris peeled off the foil and untwisted the wires that held the cork in.

"Don't let that cork pop the wrong way, Boris. You don't want to put a hole in Natalya," Petrov laughed at his own joke.

I could no longer feel my extremities.

Boris expertly popped the cork of the champagne off the side of the basket so it could plummet to the earth and knock some poor woodland creature unconscious.

He poured the fizzing drink into all four glasses, announcing, "One for each of us."

Terrific. The Captain would be drinking as well.

Keith stepped forward to take our two glasses from the Captain's hand. He turned to face me and Zak, though unaware of the latter perched next to me. Pleased with the whole experience thus far, Keith handed me my glass of champagne. I took it with shaking hands.

"To our first adventure!" Keith shouted, raising his glass high in the air and stepping toward me. The move shoved his champagne holding fist directly into Zak's face.

Zak jerked his head back.

The move knocked him off balance and, to my horror, he toppled off the side of the basket and dropped out of sight.

I screamed.

I may have screamed "Zak!", but I was so panicked I couldn't know for sure. Spinning around I lunged at the side of the basket where Zak had disappeared. My movement caused mayhem with Keith and our Russian hot air balloon crew. Their alarmed shouts blended with my own screams and everything blurred together.

In my desperation to see over the edge, I flung my upper body against the basket and dropped my champagne glass. The glass fell in slow motion, champagne cascading out of it into the sky, before it dropped right into Zak's hand.

Floating serenely about twenty feet below the balloon basket, he lay back on his wings, looking up and smiling at me.

I, on the other hand, was not so serene. Pressed hard against the basket, both arms flopping over the side so the edge of the basket jammed painfully into my armpits, I gaped at him, in shock.

"Whoa, Elsie," Keith said. "Be careful. Why don't you step away from the side?" Calm, but not totally collected, Keith's voice held an edge to it that sounded like he was questioning my sensibilities.

Heck, I was questioning my sensibilities.

Hanging my head over the side of the balloon, I took rasping breaths. My legs were too weak to hold me up, so almost all of my body weight was on my armpits where the surprisingly hard basket edge dug into them, but kept me upright.

From his vantage point below, Zak's amused expression shifted to worry. Instantly he floated up until we were face-to-face. My eyes must have been wild with terror, because Zak started speaking to me as if I was a small child.

"It's okay, Elsie. I'm okay. I didn't fall, see? I have wings!" He tried to smile, but his eyes remained troubled.

"If you're not feeling well, we have the sickness bags for that," Petrov's voice came to me from behind. They were all worried I was going to throw up, which wasn't something I could have ruled out at that point.

I felt a hand on the small of my back and hoped it was Keith's. Not that I wanted him to touch me, but would have liked it even less if Boris or Petrov were touching me.

"Do you need an air sickness bag?" Keith asked in a low voice from somewhere behind my right ear, obviously hoping that I did not.

Zak ignored whatever was going on behind me and took one of my hands in his. My racing heart slowed a little.

"No, thank you," I managed to answer, not taking my eyes off of Zak's. "I'm just...I just need a minute."

"Okay, whatever you need," Keith said. His hand patted the small of my back a few times then went away.

Quietly, oh so quietly, I whispered to Zak, "I can't move."

"You're okay, Elsie. I think you're having a panic attack, but you're going to be fine. I'm not going anywhere, okay? I'm right here. I've got your back, always."

"Can you please come back inside the basket?" I couldn't stand him floating out there in nothingness.

Zak smiled warmly. "Sure, here," he placed my now empty champagne glass into my hand and wrapped both of my hands around it, closing his own around them in a warm grip. "Can you hang on to that?"

I nodded, already feeling better knowing he was returning to the basket. As he floated closer to get back in, I stopped him with another whisper, "Wait!"

"What?"

"Please don't sit on the side again."

"Gotcha," he said.

Within moments Zak was back in the basket standing next to me. Gently, he put his arm around my back, hooking his hand underneath my arm to support my body weight. Keith and the Russians were hidden from my view as Zak stretched his wings behind me, giving me privacy. Or, at least, perceived privacy, as they could see right through him. It still made me feel better.

Warmth and light moved through my body, pushing out the fear and giving me strength. I was able to put more weight onto my legs with less wobble and was soon merely leaning on the side off the basket, not using it to keep from collapsing.

"I've got you, Elsie. You're safe. I've got your back," Zak said sweetly.

The sensation of being held by an angel was something I had

enjoyed when we roller skated and danced in my kitchen, but this time it was different. I was completely dependent on him. I knew with everything in me that if he let go of me or stepped away I was going to dissolve. I wouldn't have the energy or strength or desire, even, to remain standing.

In those moments where we existed between the earth and the sky, held up by a few meager ropes attached to a floating balloon named Natalya, where my heart and mind had threatened to leave me as I watched him fall off the basket, it was only Zak's voice and only Zak's touch that could bring me back.

Back to where I was standing on my own two feet. Back to where I could feel my body again and trust that I wasn't going to disappear forever. Back to where I was no longer afraid.

"Are you all right?" Keith asked me from somewhere behind the wall of white feathers that were Zak's wings.

Turning to face the inside of the basket, I didn't push away from Zak. Instead, I allowed him to turn with me and keep his arm around my waist. I liked it there. I wanted it there.

Keith, Petrov and Boris all seemed ill at ease, watching me for a display of unexpected behavior. I couldn't blame them, but I might be able to distract them.

With what I hoped was a nonchalant laugh, I showed Keith my empty champagne glass. "Yes, I'm fine, but I sort of spilled my drink."

"Oh! Fill the lady's glass, Boris," Petrov instructed his second in command.

"Oh, no, no, I don't think I should have any champagne, actually," I said.

Keith gave me an exaggerated frown. "It is air sickness, isn't it? I'm so sorry, I should have checked with you to make sure you would be okay on a hot air balloon flight."

"I'm fine, really. You can have my portion of the champagne."

Keith seemed pleased with that idea and they set about pouring another round as I watched. Leaning on Zak and feeling much better about everything, a familiar scent came to me. No.

That was impossible. We were high above the treetops with nothing around us.

I stole a look at Zak who grinned when I caught his eye. Checking that Keith was still preoccupied, I leaned even closer to Zak and turned so I could smell his chest, taking in a deep breath.

There it was again.

I looked up at him in surprise. His eyes twinkled merrily.

Daring one last interaction before Keith returned his attention to me, I whispered, "You smell like funnel cake!?"

twenty-five

Elsie

Even though we had what might have been the weirdest first date in the world, Keith asked me out again before dropping me off.

"I promise we'll do something a little more down-to-earth next time," he said with a laugh.

Appreciating his joke and the fact that I was back on the ground, I agreed. I didn't think it was fair to judge him on a date when he had no idea of my personal issues with adventure or the fact that my guardian angel was along for the ride.

If Zak was bothered by the second date, he didn't make it known to me. After I agreed to go and Keith left, Zak wasn't sulky or moody like he had been about the first date. He was quiet, however. But quiet in a calm, mature way. Or so it seemed at the time.

We didn't have a moment alone together to talk about anything, because I went to bed right away and the next morning I was babysitting Amelia and Abe. Then Brooke showed up to drop them off early.

"Zak! Zak!" Amelia and Abe shouted as they charged in the front door and ran to the kitchen looking for Zak.

Brooke was less enthusiastic.

"You know they talk non-stop about your friend, Zak. Is he here? They're going to be disappointed if he's not." Brooke said, peering down the hallway where her children had disappeared moments before.

"He's not," I said, ushering her into the living room in hopes of keeping her out of the kitchen.

I was going all in on the 'your small children are just crazy' vibe with Brooke. Leading her to believe that any interaction the kids had with Zak since the roller skating party was merely play-time with an imaginary friend I had created to entertain them seemed much easier to convince her of than the truth.

Plus, now that I was dating an actual human being I figured I could distract her with that information and let Zak distract the kids out of her sight in the kitchen. My sister would be happy and my niece and nephew would get to hang out with an angel. It seemed like a win-win to me.

"He's not here?" Brooke didn't seem to believe me as she sat gingerly on the edge of the couch.

"No, he's just a friend. Why would he be here all the time? I told you I made up an invisible Zak for them for fun."

"They're awfully quiet in the kitchen," Brooke said suspiciously.

"I left them some carob cookies on the table. They're probably just eating those."

Brooke made a face. "I can't believe those cookies would keep them occupied for long. They're pretty awful."

Slightly offended, I scoffed. "They love my carob cookies." Then, remembering that I needed to distract her from any idea of going to the kitchen, I said, "But I have other news."

"Yeah? What's going on?"

"I'm dating someone."

Brooke's eyes flew open. "What? A new person?"

"Yes, someone brand new."

"Who is it? What's he like?"

"His name is Keith. He's from work."

Brooke covered her mouth with her fingertips and sucked in her breath. "This is so exciting! You've already gone on a date?"

I nodded, deciding right then and there that I wasn't going to tell her about the hot air balloon incident. I wanted this to be a positive thing, not a discussion of my previous, and current, anxieties.

"Last night. And we're going on another one this week," I added.

"Who are you and what have you done with my sister?" Brooke said with a laugh.

"Why do you say that?"

Brooke gestured at me. "Here you are going on dates, roller skating, having guys friends come over and eat pizza. I mean, you're changing right in front of my eyes."

I considered her comments. "Maybe I needed a change, you know?"

Brooke nodded emphatically. "You might be right. This could be your renaissance moment. You even look better...when you take the time to get dressed."

Self consciously, I touched the jeans I was wearing. I hadn't gotten dressed up for babysitting. "You think?"

"I do. You know, it's funny, even the kids were talking about it."

"Amelia and Abe said something?"

"Yes, Amelia said it, actually."

"What did she say?"

"She said that her Aunt Elsie was so much happier now that she had Zak. She said she could see how much you liked him on your face."

My stomach clenched tight as she spoke. But my sister didn't notice.

Brooke chuckled. "Of course, she was probably picking up on your attitude to the guy at work. What was his name again?"

It took me a second to remember. "Keith. His name's Keith."

"Right, well, Keith must have been working a little magic into your life before you went out last night, because Amelia said that a couple of weeks ago."

Brooke chuckled at the charming ways of her daughter. I felt a little cringy. I didn't tell her that I hadn't even known who Keith was for more than two weeks. There was no way he had noticeably affected my mood. Zak, on the other hand, had been around several weeks.

Brooke sucked in her breath again, excited about an idea. "You should invite him to Abe's camping birthday!"

"Zak?"

Brooke gave me a confused look. "No, Keith."

"Oh, right. Keith, of course," I laughed nervously.

"It would be a perfect time to get to know him," Brooke continued with her plan for my life.

"It's a little soon for all of that, don't you think? I mean, we've only been out once so far."

"Just keep it in mind, that's all I'm saying. We have weeks to plan. But we found a really cool camping area that has all kinds of activities nearby. Fishing and canoeing, and zip lines, there's even bungee jumping."

I felt a little sick.

Brooke patted my knee. "Don't worry, nobody expects you to bungee jump. But I do expect you to bring along your new beaux." She wagged her finger at me comically.

So many thoughts were racing through my brain that I didn't notice Brooke getting up.

"I'm gonna check on the kiddos and say goodbye," she announced as she walked down the hallway.

She was too far along for me to stop her, so I followed as quickly as I could to hopefully ward off any strangeness that might come up when she found her kids enrapt by an invisible man.

When we got to the kitchen, though, Amelia and Abe were nowhere to be seen.

"Guys, I'm leaving, where are you?" Brooke called out. Sounds of children laughing filtered in from the back door.

Once again I followed Brooke, mutely stewing over what my niece had said about my happiness since Zak had come into my life.

When Brooke opened the door, we saw Amelia and Abe sitting on my Adirondack chairs completely surrounded by chirping birds. As the door opened, the birds flew up and away in a huge rush of tweets and feathers. The kids squealed in delight.

"Oh my goodness, Elsie!" Brooke exclaimed.

For a split second I thought maybe she had suddenly gained the ability to see Zak and was shocked to find a grown man with wings sitting on the deck between her kids. I held my breath.

Brooke turned to me with bright eyes and asked, "What did you do, get a bunch of bird feeders?"

I smiled. "Not exactly."

twenty-six

Elsie

"I think they're hungry," Zak told me as he came into the kitchen with Amelia and Abe close on his heels.

"We told Zak we might eat him for a snack because he smells like chocolate cake!" Abe shouted at the volume only excited young children can get away with.

"Chocolate cake? Don't you mean funnel cake?" I mused, making Zak grin.

"No, it's chocolate cake!" Amelia disagreed loudly as she jumped up and down in one place.

"Why don't you two go wash up in the bathroom and I'll fix lunch," I suggested.

Amelia and Abe raced upstairs while I pulled a bowl of grapes and the fixings for grilled cheese sandwiches out of the fridge.

"What's for lunch?" Zak grabbed a couple of grapes and popped them in his mouth.

"I thought angels don't need to eat."

"True, but, you know, I really enjoy eating." He shot a disappointed look at the carob cookies I had left on the table for the kids. "When the food is tasty."

Ignoring his diss on my favorite healthy baked snack, I asked, "What is up with your scent? Why do you smell like funnel cakes?"

He chuckled. "It comes and goes. I'm never sure when it's going to happen. Maybe I used to know how to control it, but I don't now. I do remember that I smell different to different people."

"Really? I wonder what makes it change."

He picked up another grape. "I think the scent adjusts to whatever the person smelling it likes the most."

"So, what does that mean? I like funnel cake?"

"Apparently." He smirked. "Not carob."

"Whatever, you're being a baby about the carob."

Zak pretended to ponder something. "In fact, I can't remember any time when I ever smelled like carob for anybody," he teased.

"You don't know that, you can't remember everything," I teased right back.

"That's true."

Muffled bumping and squeals of laughter came from the upstairs bathroom. Zak and I looked at the ceiling then at each other.

"Do you want me to go see what's going on up there?" he asked.

"Naw, they'll be down in a minute and we can check out the damage later."

"Are we going to take them somewhere after lunch? The park maybe?" he asked.

I paused. Was it me or did our conversation sound a little bit like we were a couple?

"We could get ice cream at that ice cream vendor by the pond," he suggested with cautiously raised eyebrows, expecting me to panic.

Funny, after the hot air balloon incident, eating ice cream in the park didn't sound very challenging at all.

"Maybe," I answered.

I was still a little freaked out at how comfortable Zak and I were together...and how much I enjoyed our mutual casual vibe. Zak was so relaxed and the feeling looked good on him. I was suddenly aware of how cute and normal he was, stealing grapes and talking about going to the park. More like a regular guy than a guardian angel. A normal guy with wings that is.

Amelia and Abe clamored down the stairs and back into the kitchen. Zak stopped them like a traffic cop.

"Did you wash your hands?" he growled in a daddy bear voice.

Amelia giggled, "Yes, we did!"

"We did, we did!" Abe shouted. "Now you show us your wings!"

I gave Zak a questioning look. "What is he talking about?"

"Zak does a wing trick," Amelia told me, breathless with excitement. "He said he would show us again if we were good."

"A wing trick?" I asked Zak.

His face turned a little red and he rubbed the back of his neck. "It's not a trick, really. I was just doing it for the kids."

Amused at his bashfulness, I joined forces with Amelia and Abe. "I want to see your trick."

Zak's face turned even more red. "No, you don't. It's no big deal. It's not even a trick."

"It's cool, Aunt Elsie," Abe reassured me.

I sat down at the table and pulled Amelia onto my lap while Abe climbed into the chair next to me. "Show us," I smiled encouragingly.

Zak agreed, a little reluctantly. He made a show of rolling his shoulders and dropping his head from side-to-side as he shook his arms out, like a fighter about to enter the ring. Even his wings got in on the action, wiggling and rustling behind him, which made the kids start to giggle.

He bent his head forward and held perfectly still, slowly lifting his arms up from his sides, reminding me of a rock star on a stage. When he looked up at me through a few locks of dark hair that had fallen into his eyes, my heart skipped a beat.

"Remember, it's not really a trick." He tried to manage my expectations.

"Just show us," I said.

"Okay, here goes." Zak looked back at the ground, stretching his wings out behind him to their full width. Or what I thought was their full width.

Surprised, I watched as his wings continued to stretch up and out, up and out, until they filled the wall behind him and reached the ceiling. Even though they were larger than I had ever seen them, they didn't thin out or look any less hefty than they always had. Maintaining thick layers of feathers from where they sprung out of his back all the way to their tips.

Speaking of feathers, something was happening with Zak's.

They were shimmering in the light. No, that wasn't right. They were moving, catching the light and reflecting it as they moved. His wings remained giant and still, but all of the feathers were shifting and moving on their own.

Amelia giggled.

"No giggling," Zak said in his papa bear voice, shooting a fake stern glance at her in my lap.

She giggled again. Abe joined in. As their giggles continued, the shaking of the feathers grew more and more pronounced. The air in the kitchen filled with the sound of countless feathers rustling and then with the faint tinkle of bells.

Amelia covered her mouth to try to contain her excited laughter. Zak gave her another stern look, which turned into a smile and a wink before he looked back at the floor to focus on finishing his trick.

The bells grew louder and louder as did the rustling. His wings glowed bright golden white, sending the light down each feather as they shook and shimmied. When the golden white light reached the end of a feather it sparkled and shot tiny rainbows into the air.

This would have been magical to watch on one or two feathers, but on the masses of feathers covering Zak's enormous wingspan, the effect was otherworldly.

I sat in stunned silence as the roar of the tinkling bells formed into notes and then into a recognizable tune, Somewhere Over the Rainbow. The bells played the first several stanzas of the song before Zak's wings shot out a massive glow of light that exploded into a wall of sparkling rainbows before quickly fading away.

Amelia and Abe cheered. Zak's wings folded back into their normal, now not so large seeming, size. And I, well, I sat there with my mouth hanging open wondering what in the heck I had just witnessed.

Zak gave me a sheepish look. "See? It's not really a trick."

"I...uh, I don't know what that was," I said. Then, so he didn't think I had hated it. "It was impressive, though, whatever you call it."

"Wasn't it fun, Aunt Elsie? Do it again, Zak!" Amelia said.

"No, I think your Aunt Elsie has seen enough and we're gonna eat lunch," Zak answered.

As I fixed the grilled cheese and Zak got the kids to help him set the table I kept reliving the sensation of watching his trick. I couldn't put my finger on it, but the whole thing had made me feel really good, inspired almost. I was reminded of the time I had seen an all white peacock show off its impressive tail.

I chuckled to myself. Just spending the weekend hanging out with my niece and nephew and my live in angel man while he puts on a freaky feather rainbow show. Nothing to see here, folks.

After lunch we did go to the park and have ice cream and we had a great time. No extra sparkles needed. I was able to navigate eating ice cream that may or may not have been breathed on by a stranger without much anxiety at all. Overall it was a really great day.

When Brooke picked up the kids, Zak stood behind me at my

front door and waved with me as she loaded them into her car. At the last moment, Amelia broke away from her mother and raced back up the steps to give me a hug.

"I love you Aunt Elsie," she said.

"I love you, too, sweetie."

She pulled away from me and ran behind me, surprising Zak by wanting a hug from him. He crouched down so she could reach around his neck.

"I love you, Zak," she said.

"Amelia, come on, honey. We have to go," Brooke called.

Amelia pulled away from Zak, but not before giving him a kiss on his cheek.

I smiled as I watched her race back out the door to her mother. She was such a sweet kid. They both were. I was lucky to have them in my life.

I was going to share this thought with Zak, but as I closed the door and turned to face him, I was stopped short by his expression.

He looked stricken. Pale. He was staring right at me, but didn't see me at all.

"Zak, what's wrong?"

twenty-seven

Zak

It came back to me all at once.

A flood of images and sounds...and feelings. Everything racing through my head in an instant, but in some weird twist of supernatural bizarreness, also in slow motion.

I couldn't move. I couldn't talk. I couldn't answer Elsie. Heck, I could barely hear her over the explosion of noise in my ears. Every memory of my life coming at me in a single moment, overwhelming all of my senses.

Not only my life as a guardian angel.

The memories of my life as a human.

Me. Zak. My life as a man.

Elsie was freaking out. "Zak, what's wrong? What's happening?"

I heard a gasping sound. Then I realized it was me trying to breathe.

"Jeez, sit down. Lay on the couch." Elsie grabbed my arm and tried to move me.

But I couldn't move. The memories were too much. I decided to try not to control them, just let them roar through me. I stopped attempting to see or make sense of anything. It was easier if they swept across my soul like a massive storm of destruction.

Some of them, however, stood out.

"Zak, tell me what's happening. What can I do?" Elsie demanded.

She was sitting next to me. I was on the couch. Damned if she hadn't moved me there without me noticing. When I looked into her eyes, those beautiful brown eyes, they were full of fear and worry. I couldn't be the cause of her freaking out. I had to explain.

"I remembered," I said.

"What did you remember?"

"Everything."

Surprise and concern on her face. Her hand on my shoulder for support. I kept going, letting the scenes of my life that I had managed to grasp onto and keep straight in my mind come out into the open.

"The girl. The little girl dancing on her father's shoes. That was my sister. My baby sister, Grace."

"Your sister?"

"And it wasn't her father she was dancing with. It was me."

She gasped. Elsie's eyes searched mine for the answer she had already realized. "You're not an angel?"

"No, I am an angel now. I wasn't then."

Eyes wide, she didn't say a word. I had to keep talking before I forgot again. I wanted to get as much on record as possible in case it all slipped away.

"My Dad died when I was really young. He was sick. We weren't well off, not at all. It was just me and my Mom against the world.

Grace came after my Mom remarried. I had already left high school. Not graduated, just dropped out. I got a job working on cars when I was sixteen and stopped going to school."

Elsie watched me in stunned silence, but she kept her hand on my shoulder. It helped, you know? To have her there. To have someone who cared.

"Technically, Grace was my half sister. But she was amazing. So small and pink and helpless. I loved her with my whole heart from the first moment I laid eyes on her."

I could tell Elsie wanted to know more about Grace. And I wanted to tell her, but there was something else I had to get out first. Something that had to do with her. With us.

"My Mom's new husband wasn't a great provider. I never liked him that much. They never had enough money for anything. I was living on my own, but I used to bring my Mom money for diapers and formula on the sly to help out.

"I drank too much. Partied too hard. Had too many girl-friends. I liked to go fast. Motorcycles, muscle cars, whatever got my adrenaline going. I never thought about tomorrow."

I paused. I needed to take a breath before telling Elsie the end of my story.

"Oh, Zak." Her brow was wrinkled with worry.

I had to look away from her. I couldn't stand to see her sweet face twisted with anxiety. So I stared at my feet. When I told her my final memory, the memory of the end of my life as a man, my voice cracked.

"Right after Grace turned eight, my Mom got sick." A hard knot formed in my throat, threatening to silence my story. I swallowed hard and continued. "She died six weeks later. Cancer. She'd been in pain for so long and never said a word to anybody. But then, nobody had ever asked."

Elsie made a sympathetic sound. I didn't dare look up at her.

"Her husband, Grace's dad, moved away to live near his relatives. He took Grace with him. He said he would send me their new address, but he never did. Grace was gone. My Mom was gone. Nothing mattered. I didn't care about anything."

I paused. My hands were on my knees, clenched into fists, as the final moments of my life raced over and over again across my mind's eye.

"I was drinking. I couldn't even tell you how much. A helluva lot. I got behind the wheel and drove. Drove as fast as I could up into the foothills. Faster and faster. Until I lost control where the edge of the road dropped off into a deep gulley. That's where my life as I knew it ended."

twenty-eight

Elsie

I didn't know what to say. I could barely wrap my brain around what Zak had just told me.

He wasn't an angel!? I mean, obviously, he was an angel. He was sitting right there on my couch with huge angel wings on his back. And he had demonstrated remarkable abilities like flying through the air and walking through solid objects. There was all kinds of evidence of his *angel-ness*.

But he hadn't always been that way.

He used to be a man. A living breathing human being, just like me.

"Zak...I'm...I'm speechless," I told him.

He looked up from where he had been staring at his feet. The color hadn't returned to his face. His eyes were vacant of their normal good humor and, I noted, his usual concern for me.

No wonder. If I was stunned at his news, what must he be feeling?

Heat resonated up from his back through the fabric of his

flannel shirt to my hand. His muscles tensed underneath my fingers as the strong emotions his memories had brought up seemed to move through his body.

The realization of where he had come from, what he had been through, everything he had lost, was transforming him somehow. Not that he was changing in front of my eyes and wasn't an angel anymore, nothing that dramatic. It was my perspective that was shifting. The way I viewed him was transforming.

Since the moment he had frozen my cell phone in mid-air the night that we met, I had always thought of him as something otherworldly. A being wholly different from me.

At first I thought that being was an imaginary person I had created in my mind. Then I came to believe he was an angel. A supernatural Zak sent from the rulers of the universe to take care of me.

But that wasn't the truth.

Zak was a real person. Or at least he had been at one time.

What did that mean for him? What did it mean for us?

Us.

The word reverberated through my heart. If he was actually human, was there an us?

"I'm sorry, Elsie," he said quietly.

Brought back from my own thoughts, I leaned into him to hear better. "Sorry? Sorry for what?"

"All of this is my fault. Your life is a big mess because of me. It doesn't have anything to do with you being too careful or boring."

Boring? A little harsh, but I tried not to allow his choice of words to throw me. He was in distress after all.

Patting his back in an attempt to offer him comfort, I said, "My life's not a big mess. You haven't ruined anything."

He scoffed at me and threw up his hands. "You're stuck with a big fat failure of a guardian angel. I'm not even a real angel. They sent me here on a kind of last chance to get it right deal."

"A last chance?"

"They told me I could take the guardian angel gig to try and make up for throwing my human life away."

"Who are 'they' exactly?"

Zak swept one arm upward toward the ceiling. "Esme, for one. That's the rainbow lady."

"Esme," I repeated the name carefully.

"And Haniel and Neriah, among others."

"Okay," I was taking controlled breaths, trying to keep my own emotions from going loopy. Here was Zak, my guardian angel who used to be a living breathing man, talking about other angels by name as if this was the most normal thing in the world to do.

"They all said since I had basically wasted my chance at life that I could try to do better by helping someone else." He flicked his gaze to me. "And you know how that turned out."

"I'm sorry, I'm just so confused. They turn people into angels? That's a thing?"

"I guess so." He leaned forward and put his face in his hands, rubbing his palms up and down on his cheeks in aggravation. "I've screwed it all up. My life. Now your life. Everything."

"Actually, I kinda thought my life was improving," I offered weakly.

"You don't have to humor me, Elsie. You'll be better off when I go back to wherever I came from."

That wasn't what I had been thinking, but before I could tell him, he had another thought.

"Where do you think they'll send me? Will I die forever this time?"

My eyes flew open. "No, they wouldn't do that! What was the rainbow lady's name again?"

"Esme?"

"Esme wouldn't do that, would she?" It was an alarming idea. But, really, what did either of us know about what Esme or the other angels or God or the universe would do at any given moment? We knew squat, that's what.

Zak stood quickly and paced up and down the living room a few times. Several feathers flew off of his wings and drifted to the floor.

"You're molting," I told him, knowing this probably wasn't the best news, but figuring he should know.

He turned and looked at the fallen feathers with dismay. When he lifted his gaze to mine it was full of sadness. "I don't know what to do. I don't want to die."

His words squeezed my heart and I blinked furiously to fight back tears. Something took hold of me and I jumped up and went to him, wrapping my arms around his neck. He hesitated for an instant then I felt his strong arms hugging me back.

The tears I had kept at bay came, but I got myself under control after a few long moments. When I stepped away from him, I kept my hands on his shoulders and looked him square in the eye.

"We are not going to let that happen. We have all of this new information now. That's got to help. We will figure something out."

His eyes wet, Zak nodded and cleared his throat. "Okay, where do you think we should start?"

"What was it that Esme said you had to do to put things back in balance?"

"She said I had to make a positive difference in the life I had been entrusted."

"And you don't think she means my life, do you?"

Zak shook his head. "No, I think she means mine."

"Okay, you were trusted with your life and..."

"And I wasted it. Threw it away," his voice was sober, but not completely morose. I took that as a good sign.

"So you have to make a positive difference in your life?" I said with more than a little uncertainty.

"The life I've been entrusted." Zak repeated. He didn't seem to understand it any better than I did.

"Jeez, that's not cryptic at all, is it?" I asked sarcastically.

Zak sighed. "I know. I don't understand what it means." He looked at me with a wan smile. "And I think you might be a little too exhausted to figure it out tonight. It's late already, Elsie. Why don't you go to bed. I'll try to relax and think about what it might mean. We can go over it again in the morning."

"Bed?" I glanced out my front window and was surprised to see that it was already dusk. The time had flown by since Amelia and Abe left.

Amelia. It was Amelia kissing Zak on the cheek and telling him she loved him that had triggered all of his memories. Sadness squeezed my heart again. I wanted to ask him more about Grace and tell him I was so sorry he had lost her as well as his parents. I understood that kind of loss.

But it was late and he was right, I was tired. It had been a long day and I would probably think better after I slept.

We said goodnight and I went upstairs. Knowing that Zak was awake somewhere in the house while I crawled into bed and closed my eyes was heartbreaking. Reliving all of those memories had to be hard and not being able to drift off into sleep for some relief would be even harder.

I felt for him and wished I could stay up all night with him, but as soon as my head hit the pillow I was out. He would have to deal with the memory of his human life on his own.

twenty-nine

Zak

"Esme!"

I called into the rainbow glow. I wasn't in the mood to wait for her to show up. I wanted, no, I *needed* to get my life and Elsie's life back to normal. Or at least not this crazy mixed up unbalanced bologna I had gotten us into.

"Esme, are you there?"

"I am here, ZakZakiel," Esme answered, the sound humming all around me.

"I remembered. I remembered everything. I remembered who I am." When there was no response I realized I hadn't known exactly what I expected her to say, but saying nothing was not acceptable. "I remember my life. My Mom and Dad...and Grace."

I tried not to get choked up. Not sure how angels viewed a converted angel who got too emotional.

"You know who you were," Esme answered, finally. "And you remember how you became who you are now."

"Yes, I remember my life and my death. And that you allowed me to become a guardian angel."

"That is good. You can restore the balance."

"Well, you see, that's what I don't quite get."

"You're confused."

"Yes, Esme, I'm very confused. I could use some help here. I need to fix what I did so Elsie can get back to her life."

There was a long pause, then, "You believe Elsie should go back to her life the way it was before she knew you existed?"

"Yes, don't you?"

Another long pause, but this time a figure materialized out of the rainbow light. A small woman with a square figure and white hair cut short. She wore a flowing white robe and gold rimmed glasses. The feathers on her wings were tipped with gold.

"ZakZakiel," she smiled warmly.

"Hi," I felt better seeing her. Not quite so lost. "It's good to see you."

"It's good to see you, too."

"What am I supposed to do about this balance thing? Can you give me details? Some guidance? We're at a total loss."

"We?"

"Elsie wants to help. You know, she wants to get me out of her hair."

One eyebrow on Esme's serene face raised discreetly. "Are you sure?"

I stared at her, my heart rate increasing as each moment went by....what did she mean was I sure?

"I, um, what?"

"Are you sure Elsie wants you out of her hair? Are you sure you want everything to go back the way it was?" She asked the questions so matter-of-fact, like there was another option.

Wait. Was there another option?

"Do I have a choice?"

Esme smiled quietly. "There is always a choice ZakZakiel."

"All right, what are my choices?"

Esme's smile grew. "Your first choice is to return to being Elsie's guardian angel, but remain unseen and unheard by her. Your second choice is to be reassigned to a new human who is in need of a guardian angel."

"Oh," I tilted my head from side-to-side, weighing my options, though it wasn't much of a choice for me. I didn't want to leave Elsie, even if I couldn't be a real part of her life anymore. I couldn't imagine a day going by where I didn't get to see her. "I want to stay with Elsie."

Esme raised her eyebrow again. She seemed kinda skeptical for an angel. "You do? Even after what you did to try and escape her?"

My stomach knotted up and I averted my gaze. "That was a mistake. I won't ever be able to change what I did, but I regret it." I turned back to Esme. "I'm asking for forgiveness."

Esme's brow pinched and she looked at me with kind eyes. "Forgive yourself, ZakZakiel. You don't need to seek forgiveness from anywhere else."

The knot in my stomach moved up into my throat and I had to blink back tears. I nodded, unable to speak.

Esme smiled again. "And there is now a third choice."

It took a second for her words to register in my mind. I cleared my throat. "A third choice?"

She nodded, eyeing me for my reaction. I tried to play it cool, but I couldn't help but hope she had saved the best for last.

"Your third choice is a second chance at being human."

All of the sensation rushed out of my arms and legs. I felt like I was swaying, though I didn't know if we were standing on anything solid to begin with. I tried to speak, but my voice came out as air, like I'd been punched in the gut.

I shook the dizziness out of my head and tried again, "I could be human again?"

Esme pressed her lips together, suppressing what might have been mirth, and nodded. "Yes. Your third option is to become human again."

Shock and joy shot through my body and I let out a surprised laugh. "Are you serious!?"

Esme nodded again, obviously enjoying my excitement.

"How would that work? Do I go all the way back and get born somewhere?" As exciting as the idea of being human again was, I wasn't completely thrilled at the idea of having to grow up all over again.

"You would be made wholly human now. You would be as you are here, but a human. You would be Zak."

"Wow, that would be amazing."

"There is one catch."

"Oh?" Again, the knot in my stomach.

"With your human form comes everything about being human. Including mortality."

"Oh." That felt heavy. I hadn't had to think about mortality for a while. Even when I'd gotten so depressed and tried to off myself in the kitchen, deep down I had known there was no real way for me to actually die.

"You'll have to think about what you want," Esme said.

"I don't have to decide right now?" The urgency I had been feeling ebbed and a sense of relief rushed in.

Esme chuckled and shook her head 'no'. "You can't choose yet anyway."

"I can't?" Disappointment replaced the relief. "Why not?"

Esme leveled her gold framed gaze at me with an all knowing smile and said, "Everything in balance, ZakZakiel. You must consider your options carefully."

An instant later I landed in Elsie's living room with a thud.

I was still reeling from Esme's news that I could choose to become human. Then she hits me with some more nonsense about balance and dumps me back into Elsie's house?

I was not happy, but I didn't have time to be aggravated or try to get back in touch with Esme, because Elsie was calling me from upstairs. Her voice was high pitched and frantic. Like something was really, really wrong.

thirty

Elsie

Standing in the middle of my bedroom, holding my cell phone at an awkward angle away from my body, I was too freaked out to think straight. I hadn't been able to move since I hung up from Brooke's phone call. I had been calling for Zak, but he wasn't there, which added to the panic buzzing through my body.

Then, suddenly, he appeared. All six foot whatever of him, flannel shirt and bulking wings filling the doorway to my bedroom.

"Zak, where have you been? We have to go!" I practically shouted.

"What's the matter?" He came to my side.

My whole body was trembling so hard I could barely say the words. Brooke's urgent voice still echoed through my head, so I repeated what she had said.

"Aunt Millie had a heart attack. She's in the hospital. We have to get there!" My voice rose in pitch with each sentence.

Surprised, but steadier than I was, Zak said, "Let's go. Do you want to put on clothes?"

I looked down at my cotton pajama bottoms and T-shirt, my brain numb. I didn't know what to do. I looked at my cell phone as if it might have a good idea.

"Here," Zak gently pried my cell from my hand and gave me instructions. "I'll get your purse and keys. You put on some jeans, a shirt and some shoes and we'll go." I was glad he reminded me about the shoes. I may have forgotten.

A few minutes later we were at my car. Zak handed me my keys, which he had dug out of my purse. My hand was shaking when I took them.

He paused. "I don't think you should drive like this."

"How will we get there if I don't drive?"

Five minutes later I was strapped into the passenger seat while Zak drove my car to the hospital. He had moved the seat all the way back and tilted the steering wheel as high as it would go, but he and his wings still looked awful squished.

"It's better than you driving in your condition," he had argued.

"Won't it look suspicious if nobody can see you driving the car?"

"It's the middle of the night. There's hardly anybody around."

I agreed, I was in no condition to operate a vehicle, but I still wondered what would happen if we got pulled over. But really, that was the least of my worries. My main concern was Aunt Millie and how she was doing.

Are you here yet?

Brooke's text buzzed through. I typed in that I would be there in about ten minutes, almost using the word 'we' instead of 'I', which could have been confusing.

"How are you doing?" Zak glanced at me anxiously from his position hunched over the steering wheel.

"I just want to get there."

"Right, right," Zak murmured, purposefully using the turn signal before making a right turn onto the street that would take us to the hospital. "She's fine. She's going to be fine."

"Do you know that? Can you see that somewhere?" I looked at the space above his head as if he might have a hidden halo that acted as an antennae where he picked up important news.

"No, no, I just mean, she's going to be okay. It's all going to be fine." He seemed a little uncomfortable. Maybe it was his awkward driving position.

When we got to the hospital he stayed by my side helping me navigate the near empty hallways and elevators until we arrived at the appropriate waiting room. I was glad to have him near me, making sure I went the right way. What in the world did people do when they didn't have someone level headed to help them at times like these?

"Elsie?" Brooke's tired voice cracked a little bit when I walked into the waiting area. Her dark hair was pulled back with a scrunchie and she looked as thrown together as I did, ragged with worry.

She stood and I hurried to her. We hugged and didn't let go. Brooke's thin frame felt light enough to fly away so I squeezed tighter. That's when she started crying.

"Oh, Elsie," Brooke sobbed into my hair.

"Shhh, it's okay," I whispered, taking a page from Zak's playbook of wishful speaking. I leaned back so I could look into her face. "Come on, let's sit down," I suggested. She truly looked awful and I was worried she might faint if we stood there too long. "Where's Brady?"

Brooke wiped her nose with some tissues she had ready in her hand. "As soon as his Mom gets to our house to watch the kids he'll be back."

"Good," I said, guiding her down into a chair and settling into the one next to her. Zak sat a few chairs down so his wings would fit.

Brooke filled me in on what had happened. Aunt Millie had

called and woke her up and said she felt like an elephant was standing on her chest and she couldn't breathe. Brady called an ambulance while Brooke tried to calm Aunt Millie down. Brady drove her and the kids to meet the ambulance at the emergency room. They had immediately admitted Aunt Millie saying she was having a cardiac arrest. Brady took the kids home so his Mom could watch them.

"They're supposed to find me in this waiting area and let me know what room number she's in so we can be with her," Brooke said through sniffles.

"Good," I said, trying to stay strong for my sister and Aunt Millie. But her words echoed through my body. I felt as weightless as Brooke had seemed to me when we hugged.

Brooke's phone rang and she answered. It was Brady. They exchanged a few words then Brooke stood to leave, saying to me, "I'll be right back. I'm going to go meet him so he can find his way up here without getting lost."

I nodded and watched her go. The odd weightlessness remained and I stared into the middle distance.

Zak leaned over and nudged me gently with his elbow. "You all right?"

Before I could think of a response a nurse came into the waiting area and looked at me. "Brooke Coleman?"

"No, I'm her sister."

"Your aunt can see you now. I can show you to her room," the nurse offered.

Zak followed me as I followed the nurse to Aunt Millie's room. As soon as I walked in I couldn't contain my tears. She looked so small propped up in that big hospital bed, wires attached to her, beeping monitors everywhere, an IV bag dripping fluids into her arm.

She smiled as I rushed in and hugged her. "Aunt Millie, how are you feeling? Are you okay?"

"There, there, sweetie, I'm just fine." Her voice was a little weak, but she was alert, which was wonderful. She patted the top of my head, knowing I was crying and giving me quiet permission to let it out.

"I'm sorry," I blubbered. "I wanted to come to help you since you're sick. Not cry like a baby."

"Now, now Elsie, you're just fine. It's upsetting when someone's in the hospital. It's okay to cry."

I managed to get myself under control and stood up, keeping one hand holding hers while Aunt Millie gave me some of the tissues off of her hospital stand with her free hand.

"Wipe your tears, sweetie. I'm glad you came." She smiled her darling old lady smile at me then looked past me at the open door. "And I see you brought your friend with you, too."

I froze. All thoughts of the beeping monitors and worries about Aunt Millie's health fell away. I stared at her.

"What?" I asked, the question nothing more than a whisper.

Aunt Millie, still smiling, beaming actually, lifted her hand in a little wave, beckoning whoever was behind me to come into the room.

thirty-one

Elsie

"Hello, Zak," Aunt Millie said. "Please come in."

I watched Zak in disbelief as he entered the room. I had to lean on Aunt Millie's bed for support.

Zak kept his eyes trained on Aunt Millie, his expression soft and calm, a genuine smile on his lips.

"Hello Millie," he said as he joined me at her bedside.

"You're taking good care of Elsie, I see," Aunt Millie said.

"I'm trying." His eyes twinkled.

"I–I–I...y-y-you..." I had found my voice, but couldn't keep from stuttering. My surprise was too complete. Finally, I managed to blurt out, "Y-you can see him?" I swept my gaze up to the tip of his wings then back down to Aunt Millie. "All of him?"

"Yes, sweetie, I can."

I coughed out a laugh, then another. "Oh my God! I can't believe this!"

"How are you feeling?" Zak asked Aunt Millie, apparently unperturbed at the fact that she could actually see him.

"Not bad considering everything," Aunt Millie answered.

They ignored me as they discussed her hospital stay and I gawked at each of them in turn. Was Aunt Millie really completely blasé about seeing an angel? Was Zak really totally unsurprised that he was visible to her?

Unless...what had Aunt Millie said? You've brought your friend? How did she know Zak was here with me? Why wouldn't she just think he was a random angel standing in the doorway to her hospital room?

I gasped. The sound brought their conversation to a halt and they turned their attention to me.

"You saw him at the roller rink?" I asked.

Aunt Millie nodded. "Yes, I saw him. So did your niece and nephew and all of the other children. Amelia and Abe talk about him all the time."

"I knew the kids saw him, but...but you? You didn't say anything."

Aunt Millie chuckled. "I could tell you didn't want everyone to know. Besides, you had an angel with you. That could only be a good thing, right?"

I smacked my hand to my forehead and left it there hoping I could press sanity back into my brain.

"You were having such a good time, Elsie. Roller skating! I never thought I'd see the day when you would go roller skating." Aunt Millie chuckled again, giving a nod of approval to Zak. "You're good for her."

Zak nearly blushed, looking down at the floor bashfully, avoiding eye contact with me completely.

I stared at him. Something wasn't right.

He looked up and I caught a wisp of guilt on his face. Flicking his eyes quickly from mine, he kept them focused on Aunt Millie as my suspicions mounted.

What would Zak have to feel guilty about? There was something he wasn't telling me and I wanted to know what it was.

The sound of my cell phone buzzing jolted me out my own thoughts. It was Brooke.

"Hey," I said, still watching Zak.

"We're in the waiting area. Are you with Aunt Millie?" Brooke asked.

"Yes, room 423."

"Okay, we'll be there soon."

I hit the End Call button. Slowly, deliberately, I put my phone in the pocket of my jeans, never taking my eyes off of Zak. He tried to avoid glancing at me, but I was sure he could feel my stare boring into him.

"Brooke and Brady are on their way," I said.

"Oh good, I hope she's not too worried," Aunt Millie fussed.

Jerking my head toward the corner of the room, I spoke to Zak under my breath, "Can I talk to you?"

"Sure," he answered, smiling bravely. "Excuse us for a minute, Millie?"

Aunt Millie nodded her consent. Just as we stepped away, Brooke and Brady came into the room and went to Aunt Millie's bedside, greeting her with a flurry of questions.

Glad for the distraction, I whispered to Zak, "You knew she saw you at the roller rink, didn't you?"

Again, guilt tinted his expression. He shoved his hands into his pockets and drew his shoulders up to his ears in an attempt at looking innocent, but he didn't deny it.

Incredulous, I fought the urge to raise my voice. Brooke and Brady were still totally wrapped up in talking to Aunt Millie, but me yelling at an invisible Zak in the corner of the hospital room would not go unnoticed.

"Why didn't you tell me?"

"I didn't know how to tell you."

What was that supposed to mean? He certainly wasn't shy about telling me every other thing under the sun, why would the fact that my Aunt Millie had been able to see him be so difficult?

I gave him the most angry and confused glare I could muster without drawing Brooke and Brady's attention.

Zak didn't budge. He didn't look away. The guilt that had lingered in his eyes was replaced by sadness as he waited for me to connect the dots.

Then it came to me.

My heart stopped and I sucked in my breath. An icy cold trickled through my veins and reached my heart, freezing it from the inside out and filling it with grief. The only people who could see an angel were those who were nearer to God. Young children...and people who were close to death.

All noise ceased. I turned to look at Aunt Millie. A move that only took a moment, but felt like an eternity. Brooke was adjusting Aunt Millie's covers and chattering nervously while Brady kept his hand on his wife's back, offering his support. Aunt Millie was looking past both of them, directly at me.

I knew instantly. The sad smile in her eyes said it all. Aunt Millie was going to die. Soon.

"Elsie. Elsie." The words emerged from the oppressive silence that had fallen around me.

Brooke was looking at me sternly. Her mouth was moving. Was she talking to me?

"Elsie!" Brooke snapped. The noise finally broke through.

"What?" I managed to answer.

"Come over here, Aunt Millie wants to tell us something."

I tried breathing, but I couldn't take in air. The hospital room started to shrink, like I was seeing it through a tunnel.

Zak put his hand on my back. Air rushed into my lungs. The tunnel vision went away. With his support, I was able to walk to the side of Aunt Millie's bed. Brooke stood on the other side with Brady standing dutifully beside her.

"Now, girls, I want to tell you something," Aunt Millie started.

"I think you should rest, don't use up your strength," Brooke said, her voice laced with a frenetic bossiness that was her go to when she was terrified.

Aunt Millie reached over and held Brooke's hand, then she offered me her other hand. I took hold of it carefully, her fingers were cool and light.

"I'm plenty strong to say what I want to say," Aunt Millie said. Brooke fell silent. "I want you both to know that it has been the greatest joy of my life to watch you grow up into the wonderful women that you are."

My throat clenched tight and hot tears filled my eyes. I didn't dare look at anything except Aunt Millie's sweet little old lady face.

"I know your parents would have been so proud of you. They loved you dearly, you know that. And I have loved you dearly, too. I couldn't have been any prouder of my very own children if I had them." She smiled at all of us. "You too, Brady. You're like a son to me, you know. And then there's Abe and Amelia," she chuckled with delight at the mere thought of the children. "They are the dearest little imps I have ever seen. I couldn't have been more blessed than to be your aunt and their great-aunt."

"Oh, Aunt Millie," Brooke broke down into sobs.

Aunt Millie shook Brooke's hand gently. "Brooke, try not to be upset. Everything will work out, you'll see." She looked at Brady. "Will you take her to get a nice cup of coffee? Maybe bring us all a coffee?"

"Sure, Aunt Millie, we'll be back in a few minutes," Brady answered, his voice gruff with emotion. He put his arm around Brooke's shoulder and guided her out of the room.

Aunt Millie turned her gaze meaningfully to Zak, who nodded and, without a word, stepped into the hallway just outside the door.

"I have something to tell you, Elsie," Aunt Millie said.

I, too, was crying, and could only nod in response.

"I saw you roller skating with Zak. I saw the joy in your eyes,

Elsie. Don't let go of anyone who can bring you that kind of joy. I don't care if they're an angel or a ghost or a merman!" She let out a little laugh at her own joke, then patted my hand. "Squeeze what joy you can out of this life, sweetie. That's what I want you to remember."

thirty-two

Elsie

We had almost two weeks to say goodbye. The first week was full of doctors and tests, visiting hours, and flower and balloon deliveries. The second was full of laughter and tears.

Aunt Millie faced the end of her life with love and good humor. Brooke brought photo albums to the hospital from Aunt Millie's house and she told us stories of our parents when they were young. We talked about all of our memories growing up with her. Amelia and Abe visited often and brought her little cards made with brightly colored construction paper and notes written in precious wiggly block lettering.

She even helped us plan her funeral. Wanting to be sure we played music she would like and didn't spend too much on flower arrangements.

"I would rather you donate money to charities, girls," she told us, her voice weaker than it had been when she first arrived in the hospital. "Or spend money on the kids. Take them somewhere fun, somewhere they can be young and carefree."

"We're going to have flowers, Aunt Millie," Brooke disagreed politely.

Aunt Millie chuckled and patted Brooke's hand. "Okay, okay, I just would rather think of you all having a beautiful time together after I'm gone. Not spending money for an expensive funeral."

I was sitting on the other side of Aunt Millie's bed. Brooke looked at me, her lips pressed tightly together to keep from crying, her eyes full of pain.

"We'll do both, how about that?" I said, trying to be helpful. "Maybe what we should do right now is find out if we can spring you out of here. Are you tired of being in the hospital?" I knew I was tired of seeing my aunt slowly slipping away surrounded by beeping monitors in a depressing hospital environment. If her time was limited wouldn't she be better off at hospice?

"Oh, I would like to go home, Elsie. I would feel better at home," she said, her face brightening.

Home. That was the perfect idea. I looked at Brooke, certain she would do better through this whole process if she had a project. "Let's get her home."

Sisters united, we used all of our organizational and administrative skills, which were plentiful, to get Aunt Millie released from the hospital seven days after she had been admitted.

With hearts slightly less heavy, we helped her settle back into her house where she could spend whatever time she had left comfortable and happy. Brooke and I took turns caring for her needs and coordinated whatever care beyond our abilities with an at-home nurse.

In the end our aunt's heart, as welcoming and kind as it had always been, proved to be too far gone for modern medicine to repair. Aunt Millie passed away on a rainy afternoon sitting in her sunroom looking out the window at her garden. I was there, as was Brooke, Brady, Abe, Amelia, and Zak.

I wished Brooke could have seen Zak then. Seated on a high stool out of the way, up against the glass wall of the sunroom, trees and flowers of the garden stretching out behind him, he looked positively statuesque. I think she would have been impressed.

The somberness of the end of Aunt Millie's life had given him a grace I hadn't noticed before. A seriousness of duty that made him seem a little like a sentry keeping guard over her, with his great white wings offering her a view of heaven that awaited after her mortal life.

I did think Aunt Millie was comforted by his presence. As were Abe and Amelia, though they didn't pay much attention to him. They were wrapped up in loving on Aunt Millie, laying in her lap and holding her hand with their adorable little child hands.

I was comforted by Zak's presence too, but there was still something off between us. I was so tired during those two weeks and we barely spoke of anything other than Aunt Millie when we were alone. I couldn't get rid of the feeling that there might be other important details he wasn't telling me.

Aunt Millie's funeral came and went. Just as she had said it would. As Zak had known it would while we roller skated at Amelia's birthday party. A small piece of me was having a hard time forgiving him for not telling me that he had suspected she was near the end of her life, but I was too full of grief to bring it up.

After her funeral, which was tasteful, but modest, as she had wanted, I stood at the side of her grave in my best black dress. Zak on one side. Keith on the other.

I had allowed Keith to take me out to a short lunch instead of our scheduled dinner date the week Aunt Millie was in the hospital. In my grief I had told him about her illness.

"I'm so sorry to hear that, Elsie," he had said, his handsome face crimping with concern. "How are you doing?"

I tried to shrug off the weight of it all. "I'm holding up."

Keith watched me for a long moment then reached out and took my hand. "I understand that we haven't been going out for very long at all, but I would like to do what I can for you at this difficult time."

I smiled weakly. "That's nice, Keith, but I don't think I need anything."

He returned my smile with an empathetic one of his own. "Forgive me if this is too personal, but I have lost loved ones. You may not be capable of verbalizing your needs at this time. If you don't mind I would be happy to offer occasional assistance throughout your troubles. If you want to accept it you can. If you don't, you owe me no explanation. How does that sound?"

It sounded competent, well thought out, and reassuring.

"That sounds okay," I said, glancing quickly at Zak before focusing back on Keith. My emotions were too frazzled to deal with any objection Zak might have.

Zak had been extremely compliant and accommodating to me since Aunt Millie had gone into the hospital. He hadn't requested I do any more challenges to change my life and we had stopped discussing how we were going to get him returned to his world. He became a permanent silent fixture in the back corner of every room I was in, invisible to everyone else except Aunt Millie and the kids.

Keith did what he said he was going to do, calling or texting with offers of assistance over the days that followed. He was always kind and proper in our interactions. He even went to his uncle on my behalf so I wouldn't be burdened with having to speak to work about taking so much time off.

When he found out the time and day of the funeral Keith offered to escort me, be my driver, and help wherever he could. What a relief, handing over responsibility of getting to and from the funeral home on the day to someone else. Zak probably would have offered, but I couldn't let him drive me around. An invisible driver would be noticed in the middle of the day. Besides with Keith offering there was no need.

I was struggling with Zak's presence. Him not confiding in me about Aunt Millie being able to see him at the roller rink gnawed at the back of my mind. Every time I looked at him it stirred up feelings of mistrust. And he was so quiet. So...passive. Everything felt wrong.

I didn't like not trusting Zak. It made me sad and I felt him growing more and more distant every day. Little by little, I found myself turning to Keith for support instead.

I stayed at the side of Aunt Millie's grave until all of the guests had gone. Brooke and Brady had taken the kids back to the limo that had brought us all from the funeral home to the graveyard. I knew I needed to leave and go back with them. Go back to my life. But I couldn't get myself to turn around and walk away.

"Elsie, it's time to go," Keith told me, his voice soft and quiet.

I shook my head. "Not yet."

Keith's feet shifted. Out of the corner of my eye I could see him glancing back toward the limo.

"Can I have a minute alone?" I asked. Then, trying to soften my request, I offered him a small smile. "Then I'll be ready."

"Sure, of course. I'll tell your sister you'll be a few more minutes." Keith smiled and touched my arm then walked away.

I took a deep shuddering breath.

Without looking directly at him, I asked Zak, "Is she all right?"

He seemed surprised at the question. Then the new Zak, the one with the peaceful graceful angel vibe, answered, "Yes, she's in a good place. You don't have to worry."

"Okay," I said, then my throat choked up and all I could do was let quiet tears flow. Zak stood on. Sentry mode still engaged.

When my tears slowed and I sniffled, he discreetly handed me some tissues.

I looked down at them and glanced around the nearly empty cemetery. "Where did you get these?"

He shrugged and raised one side of his mouth in an uncertain half-smile. Something about the look on his face hit me funny and I snorted out a small laugh. Then another. I covered my mouth with my hand and looked at him, eyes wide. A cemetery was hardly the place to crack up laughing.

Zak's half-smile reached his eyes. He leaned closer to me and nudged my shoulder gently with his. "It's okay. I don't think your Aunt Millie would mind."

That added tears to my laughter and it took me a minute to get myself under control. When I was done cry-laughing, I wiped my eyes with the tissues he had given me.

In the pause after my emotional release, Zak said, "I'm sorry."

I sniffled and blew my nose. "For what?"

In a voice full of regret, he answered, "For not telling you. I should have told you."

My midsection tightened for an instant. I turned to him to say what I needed to say.

"Do you understand why I'm upset, Zak? What could have happened? She could have died that first night in the hospital and I wouldn't have had the chance to say goodbye. To tell her..."

The tightness in my body moved up through my chest and into my throat, threatening to release more tears. I bit my lip and willed the tears back down.

"It would have been awful. It's awful to not say goodbye when people leave you," I added.

Zak's head pulled back, as if my words had physically hit him in the face. Then he put his hands on my arms, forcing me to look up at him.

"I'm not going to leave you, Elsie," he said, searching my eyes to see if I believed him.

I shook my head, "You mean you can't leave me. You're stuck with me."

"No, I mean I don't want to leave you and I won't."

I gave him a tight smile then pulled away and started back toward the limo. I wanted to believe him, but something inside me wouldn't allow it.

thirty-three

Elsie

The first thing I did when I drove with Brooke to Aunt Millie's house so we could start dealing with her estate was take Now We Are Free off of her playlist.

"What are you doing?" Brooke asked from the driver's seat.

I finished clicking buttons on her phone and the deeply moving piece written by Hans Zimmer for the movie Gladiator stopped flowing out of her car speakers.

"I can't listen to that right now, Brooke. It's too much. It makes me want to collapse into a giant blubbering ball," I told her.

Zak was in the back seat and I could sense him smiling quietly at my comment.

Brooke huffed, but didn't make a move to change it back. Her playlist went to the next song, Michael Buble's When I Fall in Love. Not much better.

I gave her a look.

She noticed. "What?"

"Do you listen to anything that isn't depressing?"

"Michael Buble isn't depressing. You should see him in concert. He's really fun."

I picked up my phone and moved to disconnect hers.

"No," Brooke stopped me.

"Why not?"

"We're going to listen to my music first."

"Why can't we listen to mine?"

Brooke pressed her lips together and thought for a moment, then came up with her reason. "I'm the executor of the will and I decide on the music."

I shook my head in disbelief, but put my phone down. "I don't think that's a rule, but whatever you say." Again, I could sense Zak smiling at our conversation from the back seat.

Things had been a little better between Zak and I since the funeral. He was still staying calm and weirdly quiet, and he hadn't brought up returning to his angel realm yet, but it wasn't exactly awkward anymore. Except when Keith was around.

My phone buzzed. Speak of the devil. I read Keith's text and saw Brooke eyeing my phone trying to read it, too.

"Hey." I tilted my phone so she couldn't see it and immediately noticed Zak craning his neck behind me so he could see it. "Hey!" I said without thinking.

"I heard you the first time," Brooke said. "Sheesh."

"This is a private message," I told my sister, adding extra emphasis on the words for Zak's sake.

"What does Keith have to say today?" Brooke asked, her tone a little lighter since she was switching the conversation to my dating life.

"He's going to pick up Thai food tonight."

Brooke raised her eyebrows. "So you two are official now?"

"Is there something about eating Thai food that makes us official?"

"Not Thai specifically, but you know, it's kind of at the 'casual eat takeout at home which means we are super comfortable together' phase, right?" Brooke asked hopefully.

Zak snorted in the back seat. I ignored him.

"Did you have to tell him what to get for you?" Brooke asked.

"No, he's getting Tom Yum Soup and sautéed Ginger Chicken for me. That's what his text said."

"See! Those are your favorites! You two are practically married already."

Brooke laughed, which was nice to hear after everything we had been through, though her assumption made me cringe. A rustle of feathers and loud scoff erupted from the back seat, but I was way ahead of Zak's indignation at her comment.

"Not even close, Brooke. Not even remotely close," I said.

She gave me a knowing look and turned up the volume. We drove in silence for a while. Brooke humming to another Michael Buble song, Zak stewing in the back seat, and me wondering how my relationship with Keith had progressed so noticeably...and so quickly.

When we were almost to Aunt Millie's house, Brooke broke the silence. "I like Keith. He really takes care of you."

Her observation bothered me. And she was right, which was the most annoying part.

"I guess," I said tersely.

"What's the matter with that? What's the matter with having someone who takes care of you?" she asked.

"It's not that, not exactly."

I squirmed in my seat. Not only was I having trouble explaining my relationship with Keith to my sister, but I had to do it while Zak was shoved into the back seat just inches away from me. Close enough that I could hear him breathing. Which was also strange. Did angels really need to breathe?

"Don't you like him?" Brooke asked.

"Sure, he's nice. He's fine."

Brooke raised her eyebrows, amused. "Nice and fine. I doubt

old Keith would be thrilled with your description. So, what's wrong with him?"

"Nothing's wrong with him. He's fine. Very nice. Like I said."

Brooke laughed. "Well, I guess Keith won't be coming on the camping trip for Abe's birthday, will he?"

"I didn't say that." I didn't want to just toss Keith aside. He'd been so helpful and kind. "I don't know. I guess I'm not used to having someone around all the time, you know? He's always coming over and doing things for me or asking to take me somewhere. I don't feel like I have any time...to myself."

It was at that moment that I saw the irony of my statement. Everything Keith did that I had just complained about didn't feel so annoying to me when Zak did it. Zak was next to me literally all of the time and the person that was making me feel crowded was Keith.

"You're alone all of the time, Elsie. Maybe that's not a good thing. Not long term. Maybe you should let Keith be with you and see how it works out?"

I didn't dare look at Zak, whose non-verbal commentary had ceased. I was afraid he would think my comments about Keith being around too much applied to him. Which, oddly enough, they didn't. Zak made me laugh. He made me feel things I had never felt before. I kind of missed life being just Zak and I against the world.

"I don't know about that," I said to Brooke, trying to brush her concerns away.

We pulled into Aunt Millie's old driveway and I was relieved. I thought she would want to move on from our conversation, but I thought wrong.

Brooke put the car in park land turned off the engine then looked at me. "If I didn't know better I might think you were happier when you were pretending to bring your imaginary friend with you everywhere."

I laughed uncomfortably. "Don't be ridiculous."

Brooke watched me, concern pinching her brow. "It's not

healthy. That's all I'm saying. To depend on an imaginary friend for companionship. It's kind of sad, Elsie."

"Sadder than listening to Now We Are Free on loop forever while you drive?"

She rolled her eyes. "Okay, I'll let it go. You don't have to be mean about it."

"Let's go inside and get started. We have a lot to get done," I said, glad to get her off of the subject.

"Fine. Just one more thing. I really think you should give Keith a chance and bring him on the camping weekend. There's all kinds of things to do. You'll have more fun if you have a date."

It was my turn to roll my eyes.

"No, seriously, think about it," she said, putting her keys in her purse and opening the driver's side door. "Also I need help picking up supplies the week before, please."

"Fine," I said, hoping to appease my pushy sister, not sure about inviting Keith camping, and doing everything I could to avoid eye contact with Zak as I got out of the car.

thirty-four

Elsie

I don't know how I got through the next few weeks. There was so much going on, yet it felt like I was stuck trying to walk up a down escalator. Moving all the time, but staying in exactly the same spot.

I went to work during the week. I helped Brooke with Aunt Millie's estate on the weekend. Keith was around, a lot. Both at work and on the weekend. Zak was around all the time. Yet it seemed like I never talked to any of them about what I was really feeling.

Maybe because I wasn't feeling anything. I was numb.

Keith had taken to dropping off little gifts at my desk, which piqued Beth's interest.

"I see you've added to your collection," Beth said, admiring a small African Violet in a cute little pot that had mysteriously arrived at my desk while she had taken me to get some lunch.

"Yes, people are being sweet." I tried to act nonchalant.

Keith and I had never discussed whether or not we should

keep the fact that we were dating a secret at work. I thought it was probably a bad idea to let everyone know, seeing as he was the boss' nephew. Then again, I didn't even know if we were technically dating.

I mean, he took me out to eat sometimes, and he brought over takeout to my place sometimes, and he called and texted me to check on how I was doing, but he had never tried to kiss me. Nor I him. Sometimes I felt like I was more like a project for him to fix. Not that I could blame him. Lately I had felt pretty broken.

Maybe I wasn't broken exactly. But I definitely wasn't on my A-game anymore.

I was a woman living with her stranded guardian angel. I was grieving the loss of the aunt I had loved like a mother. And I was falling apart.

I had cancelled my cleaning and lawn care service after Zak appeared in my life. The need to keep Zak a secret had spurred that decision. Then I had been busy facing my anxieties and my house cleaning had slipped a little. After Aunt Millie passed, well, I just didn't have any interest in it anymore.

"Um, did you need this? It was on the couch." Zak held up my hairbrush.

I had just finished changing into jeans after work. We were going to the warehouse store to shop for the upcoming family camping weekend at the place Brooke had found, Camp Morningstar. Keith was coming to pick me up. I had invited him for the weekend like Brooke suggested and he insisted on shopping with us to help Brady with the heavy lifting.

I stared at the hairbrush in Zak's hand. When had I taken my hairbrush into the living room? I hadn't gone into the living room before work. Not the night before either, because I had been out to eat with Keith then gone straight to bed.

I shifted my eyes up to Zak's with growing alarm. "When was the last time I brushed my hair, Zak?"

Before he had a chance to answer I snatched the brush from him and hurried into my bathroom. Sure enough, my reflection verified my worst fears. I had the hairdo of a four-year old waif from a Charles Dickens novel. Not only that, but my makeup appeared to be two days old and I couldn't remember the last time I showered.

I dropped the brush on my bathroom vanity and it landed among a variety of tubes and bottles of makeup I had left strewn around. My toothpaste and toothbrush weren't neatly stored in my medicine cabinet, but laying haphazardly next to the sink. I hadn't even put the cap back on the toothpaste.

"Are you all right?" Zak asked.

I turned to him with my rats nest hair and questionable body hygiene, shocked and upset. "Do I look all right? I look like a child who has been abandoned in the forest and adopted by wolves."

A smile flickered through his eyes. "You don't look that bad."

I picked up my hairbrush and tried to pull it through my ratted hair where it promptly got stuck. I let go of the handle and the brush stayed put, dangling off the side of my head.

"Not that bad, huh?" My bottom lip started to tremble.

"Hey, hey," Zak bent down so he could look right into my eyes. "Come on, come sit down. I'll fix it."

I let him lead me over to the bed where he sat me down gently. He disappeared into the bathroom then reappeared carrying several spray bottles.

Without saying a word, Zak sat down beside me and extricated the hairbrush. Then he spritzed my hair with water and spray conditioner. Carefully he used a comb he must have dug out of my trashed bathroom to comb through the tangles at the end of my hair. When those were free, he worked his way up until a whole section was untangled.

I could see our reflection in my dresser mirror and I watched him silently, tears streaming slowly down my face. He started on the next section of my hair. My nose was running from crying and I sniffled. Wordlessly he handed me a tissue that he produced from somewhere unseen.

I smiled at the tissue in my hand then caught his gaze in the mirror. "My guardian angel sure is fast with the tissues. I guess that's a necessary trait when you're stuck with someone like me."

Zak didn't answer, but went back to combing my hair. "I used to brush out Grace's hair when it got too messy and my Mom couldn't find the time," he said thoughtfully.

"You did?" I tried to imagine him as a human, patiently brushing through a little girl's tangled hair. It wasn't hard to picture.

He nodded and even though he wasn't looking at me in our reflection, I could see sadness in his eyes. A powerful desire came over me. I wished I would have known him when he was human. Before all of the pain and confusion that had led to him being someone, or something, supernatural. Something far beyond me and my little world.

"There," Zak said, leaning back proudly and pulling the brush easily through my hair to show me he was finished.

"Thank you."

"No problem, it's what I'm here for–" he stopped himself and cocked his head to the side. "Actually, I don't think hair stylist is in the job description." He grinned.

"Right," I smiled, too, realizing it was the first time I had felt like smiling in several days.

"Are you really up for this tonight?"

I took a deep, cleansing breath. "I am, but I think I'm going to take a shower first."

He lifted his eyebrows and nodded. "That's probably a good idea."

"Oh, shush," I pushed his shoulder in protest. He pretended to be knocked completely over by my strength and fell, wings and all, onto the floor. I laughed out loud. "First, I'm going to text Keith and tell him we'll meet him there."

I showered, towel dried my hair, did a quick clean up of my bathroom vanity, and emerged fresher than I had felt in a while. I got dressed in my jeans, a blue hoodie, and a pair of sneakers, pulled my damp hair up into a messy pony tail and was ready to go.

When I entered the living room Zak was carefully folding a load of clean laundry I had left in a pile on my sitting chair. He turned, a sarcastic look on his face like he was about to comment on my recent housecleaning habits, but froze in place when he saw me.

His mouth was open as if he had suddenly forgotten what he was going to say. If I didn't know better I would have sworn I saw something like longing flash through his eyes, but that was ridiculous. My emotions were so out of whack these days, I was imagining crazy stuff.

"Ready?" I asked.

He snapped out of his hesitation and cleared his throat. "I was just, um, picking up a little."

I waved my hand dismissively. "We can leave it until later."

By the time we made it to Costco we were late. Keith was already off with Brady grabbing cases of soda and other drinks. Brooke had her hands full with Abe and Amelia and was glad to see me, especially when the kids ran to greet me and my imaginary friend Zak.

Over the past weeks, Brooke had become so accustomed to Amelia and Abe talking to Zak in her presence that she had warmed to the idea he was a handy entertainment device I had made up. They acted so much better when they had their imaginary friend she gave up complaining about how weird it was. Plus, she wasn't as worried about my sanity since Keith had become part of my everyday life.

"You two play with Zak while me and Aunt Elsie shop," she instructed the kids, waving into the empty aisle behind us.

"Zak's not there, Mommy," Amelia complained. "He's standing next to Aunt Elsie."

"Okay, fine, ask him to follow me and Aunt Elsie and you guys walk with him." Brooke gave me a look to say she had the situation under control.

I smiled and snuck a look at Zak to make sure he was cool with the plan. He grinned and stepped back, taking hold of Abe and Amelia's hands so they could follow me and Brooke as we pushed the giant cart.

Brooke gave me a sideways look. "You look good. Rested."

"I do?" I glanced down at my hoodie and jeans.

A knowing smile played on Brooke's mouth. "And I think I know why."

"Why?"

Brooke smacked my arm like I was teasing. "Keith's here, that's why."

I suppressed a burst of laughter. Then, to appease my big sister, I went ahead and agreed, "Right, it's because of Keith."

thirty-five

Zak

I followed Elsie and her sister through the warehouse store, dutifully babysitting Amelia and Abe, but distracted. I couldn't get my mind off of the fact that I was in love.

I had known I cared about Elsie for a while now. And ever since we danced in her kitchen I had also known for sure that I found her attractive. But that didn't mean I was in love with her.

It wasn't until she walked into the room after taking a shower, no makeup, hair not done up, wearing only a plain old pair of jeans and a sweatshirt, that I felt it. All the way down to my toes.

I had looked at Elsie in her purest form. No anxieties, no being on edge trying to do things right, completely vulnerable and open, and my heart just cinched up in my chest. I could barely breathe, let alone speak. With everything in me I knew without a doubt that I loved her...and not in a guardian angel kind of way.

Now, let's back it up a minute

First of all, as an angel, was I really capable of having these kinds of feelings? Or was all of this just remnants of my time lived

187

as a man? Second, and this was the bigger problem on my mind, my life as an angel was going to go on forever. I would continue existing long after Elsie grew old and passed away. With me being an angel our lives couldn't be combined. Not the way I wanted them to be at least.

"Zak, you like hotdogs, right?" Abe asked me.

We had approached a refrigerator aisle with shelves and shelves of cheese, lunchmeat and hotdogs.

"Sure, I like hotdogs," I said.

"Could you eat this many?" Amelia patted the glass door where several packages of bulk hotdogs were on sale.

I smiled and nodded. "48 hotdogs? No problem."

Amelia giggled.

Out of the corner of my eye I saw Brooke's husband, Brady, and Keith approach Elsie and her sister.

"Hey, how are you doing tonight, beautiful?" Keith greeted Elsie with a quick peck on the cheek that didn't even land.

What a dipstick. The guy was so...so...well dressed all the time. He had more product in his hair than Elsie kept in her bathroom. And he was wearing cologne. At the warehouse store. You could smell him a mile away. The guy really got on my nerves. He wasn't dangerous or anything, but I didn't like him just the same. He was a...a dipstick, that was the only word I could think of to describe him.

I clenched my teeth to keep from saying something out loud while the kids were listening, but I could taste bitterness as I watched him fall into step next to Elsie.

Someone was tugging on my sleeve. Amelia.

"Did you hear me?" she asked, her big brown eyes quizzical.

"No, sorry, what did you say?"

"Are you coming to Abe's birthday camp?"

"Yeah, are you coming with us to Camp Morningstar?" Abe chimed in.

"Yeah, I'll be there," I told them.

"Are you gonna go tubing and zipper lining?" Amelia asked.

I smiled, zipper lining. Maybe I could forget about Keith if I concentrated on talking to little Amelia. "I don't think so. I'll be watching you guys."

"It's zip lining, Amelia," Abe corrected her.

"Zip-per-lining," Amelia tried again to pronounce it correctly.

"Maybe Aunt Elsie will go zip lining if you go," Abe suggested.

"I don't think so." I flicked my eyes toward Elsie and Keith and admitted, a little dejectedly, "She might want to do those kinds of things with Keith, anyway."

"Keith?" Abe made a face and shook his head, refusing to believe me.

"No she won't," Amelia said.

My heart warmed a little bit, happy to know that at least Elsie's niece and nephew were on my side. Not that it would help a whole lot.

"Why wouldn't she do things with Keith?" I asked, trying to avert my eyes away from Keith's hand, which had slipped onto the small of Elsie's back as they walked.

"She doesn't like him," Amelia said with full confidence.

A glimmer of hope rose up in my heart, then dimmed again as Elsie laughed at something Keith said.

"I don't know about that, Amelia. She must like him. They go out to dinner and all of those kinds of things, don't they?"

"Yeah, but she doesn't like him. She likes you better," Amelia said.

As much as I wanted to take the word of a five-year old to be the absolute truth and run with it, I couldn't. Even though it broke my heart I could see the writing on the wall.

"Why would your Aunt Elsie go out on dates with someone she doesn't like?"

"Because she can't go with you since you're invisible," Amelia answered, somewhat frustrated with my inability to grasp what she was saying.

Abe nodded emphatically. "Aunt Elsie can't go on dates with someone who's invisible."

"Yeah, she needs to have a real person for her boyfriend," Amelia explained.

"Cause she's a grown up," Abe added, the almost 7-year old was also not sure why I was being so dense. "She can't have an invisible boyfriend, Zak."

I stopped walking. Both kids stopped as well. They were still holding my hands and looking up at me with serious faces after giving me the best advice I had ever received.

Why was I being so stupid? What had Esme told me? There's always a choice.

My heartbeat quickened as I watched Elsie and the others near the end of the aisle. The woman I loved was in reach, if only I had the nerve to do what needed to be done.

thirty-six

Elsie

Zak was acting a little odd. I noticed it as soon as we got back from the warehouse store. Maybe it had been going on during the shopping trip, but I had been too busy with other distractions to see it.

I couldn't ask him what was wrong, because Keith brought some ice cream over that he'd bought at the warehouse store to share with me. I ended up falling asleep on the couch while we watched a documentary on ice fishing. Not my first choice of movies, but it definitely helped me doze off for the night.

I woke up late in the morning and was subsequently late to work for the second time in my life. Then Keith insisted on taking me out on a 'real date' after work before we left for Camp Morningstar the next day. All the while I could tell something was on Zak's mind, but we never had a few minutes of down time when we were alone for him to say anything. Not until right before Keith picked me up for our 'real date'.

"Elsie, I need to talk to you about something," Zak said.

I had spent too long deciding what dress to wear. Keith had told me to dress up, which pushed my stress button and made it hard for me to make a decision. I had finally landed on a simple navy blue sleeveless sheath dress. The one I usually wore to dietician conferences.

"Okay, what's up?" I was at the front door looking through my coat closet where I stored my shoes when I came in the house, digging out a pair of navy blue pumps.

Zak watched me hop up and down on one foot while pulling on my shoe. He looked away from me down the hallway then back, giving his head a little shake as if he had made a decision.

"Naw, never mind. I'll tell you later," he said.

Finally completely shoed, I straightened my dress. "You can tell me now. I have a few minutes."

He shook his head again, a little more decisively. "It's okay, we can talk about it tomorrow."

"Actually, we probably can't, because we're leaving first thing tomorrow morning for Camp Morningstar and everyone's going to be around and we're going to be busy all weekend. I think you should tell me now."

He looked into my eyes for a long moment then he kind of winced and tugged at his ear nervously. There was definitely something wrong.

"Zak, what is it?" I really wished he would spit it out before Keith arrived. In truth, I sort of wished Keith wasn't coming at all so I could sit down with Zak and find out what was going on. A chill went down my spine. "Is it bad? Is something bad happening?"

"No, nothing like that. It's not bad at all...it could be good."

"Oh, okay. That's a relief. What is it?"

He shifted from one foot to the other then turned sideways, rubbing the palm of his hand across the back of his neck.

"Never mind," he said. "We can talk about it when you get back. It's not bad and it's not an emergency."

Irked that I had to go through my whole night not knowing, I pressed him for some kind of information. "Can you tell me what it's about, at least? In general?"

Zak turned his eyes on me, eyes that glimmered with something he wanted to say, but couldn't. Instead he chose to confuse me even more. "It's about us. You and me. This." He flicked his hand back and forth between us. "Me being your guardian angel. Or not. You being able to see me. Or not. Things changing...for the better, I hope."

I opened my mouth to demand he explain what he was talking about. A knock at the door interrupted me. Keith.

Zak went into silent mode again. He retreated down the hallway, which he had started to do more and more when Keith was around. But when Keith and I left the house and got into his car, Zak was nowhere to be seen.

I had grown so accustomed to Zak and his giant wings stuffed into every car I had been in for the past several months that it was a shock to my system for the back seat to be empty. I was hardly able to have a conversation with Keith for all of my double checking the back and peeking out the windows for a sign of Zak nearby.

None came.

It was the same at the restaurant.

"Don't you like escargot?" Keith asked.

I had been pushing the appetizer around on my plate, not really sure I wanted to dig into snail shells to get a tiny morsel of food, no matter how delicious Keith said they would be. They were swimming in butter, which wasn't something I ate a lot of, and the sight of it was making me queasy.

I offered Keith a weak smile. "My stomach is a little touchy today."

We were at a French restaurant. The kind that seated a limited number of tables for the evening, because each meal had several courses and lasted for over three hours. Everything smelled fantastic and I was sure Keith was paying a pretty penny for the experience, still I couldn't help but feel it was a little over the top.

Maybe I was uncouth. Maybe I was not up to a fancy French dinner. Or maybe I was a little preoccupied with Zak's sudden disappearance, so much so that I couldn't eat.

What in the heck had happened to him?

I picked up a slice of baguette out of a basket on our table and tore off a piece. Perhaps I was hungry and eating something would help. But I needed something simple. Not garden pests swimming in rich butter sauce.

Keith was watching me with a warm glow in his expression. "You look beautiful, Elsie. I'm sorry you're not feeling well. Would you like to go home?"

"No, no, let's not do that. You've already gone to so much trouble to get reservations here." I waved my piece of baguette around at the candlelit tables, each with a vase holding a single red rose, the crisply dressed wait staff, and the violinist who moved slowly around the room playing for each and ever guest. "I'm sure I'll feel better once I eat this bread."

"Whatever you like," Keith responded. He closed his eyes and bowed his head toward me briefly. He was so nice and gentlemanly. So ridiculously thoughtful and attentive. So attractive and well put together. There was nothing, absolutely nothing, wrong with the guy.

So why was I obsessing over where Zak went? Why was I wondering how long this whole dinner was going to take before I could get home and find out what he had wanted to talk to me about before I left?

I sighed and quietly shook my head. "You know, Keith, I don't understand why you've been so wonderful to me during these past weeks. I've been such a mess. I mean, look at me tonight. You've brought me to this beautiful restaurant and I'm all jittery, and distracted, and queasy. I'm still a mess."

Keith smiled, his teeth very white. "You may be a mess now, Elsie. But I met you before your recent adversity, remember? I know that eventually you will overcome all of this and be your old self again. And when that happens I want to be there to greet you."

I sat there for the longest time after Keith said those words to me. Something about the way he described our future together didn't sit right. It sounded nice, sort of, on the surface. But it didn't make me feel any better.

A pang of grief shot through my chest. Where was Zak? He would know what to say or give me a look that would make me laugh. Make me feel like I was okay and everything was going to be okay. Maybe not perfect, but okay.

I glanced around the restaurant again, hoping to see the fluttering of white feathers in the corner or smell the scent of funnel cake. But no. There was nothing like that in the whole place. Just me and Keith and candles and a rose and a plate full of snails I wasn't going to eat.

The truth was I didn't really want to be there. Maybe I didn't really want to be with Keith anywhere. I wasn't sure. I didn't think I was feeling what a potential girlfriend should feel.

Watching him pull cooked snails out of their little shells, swirl them in butter sauce, and gobble them up didn't help. But at least as we finished each course we were getting that much closer to me going home and seeing Zak.

I barely made it through the three hour French meal with my sanity. Feeling nearly frantic with worry over where Zak had gone I was a poor companion for the evening. Keith didn't mind. He was still patiently waiting for me to turn back into my old self again, which was irritating.

"Zak," I called down the empty hallway after Keith dropped me off and I had shut and locked the door. "Zak where are you?"

Hurrying around the house, turning on all the lights, checking the backyard and all of the closets, I did not find him. Did I really expect him to be hiding in a closet? I didn't know. I wasn't thinking straight. He had never been so far away that he couldn't hear me and come find me right away.

Fear for his safety started to creep into my heart. Could something have happened to him? What had he been trying to tell me before I went to that stupid French restaurant?

He had said it had to do with us.

Us.

The word reverberated more heavily through me than when Zak had used it earlier. I hadn't paused long enough to let the possible meanings sink in. We were an us? Us as in together? Or us as in stuck together in an impossible situation?

He had also been talking about being my guardian angel and me being able to see him...or not. What did that mean?

"Ugh, Elsie, why didn't you stop and listen to him?"

Angrily pulling off my dress, I changed into pajamas. My stomach growled. I hadn't eaten much at the restaurant. There was some leftover Thai food in the fridge. I had to do something while I waited for Zak to return. So I shuffled to the kitchen, grabbed the takeout containers, and carried them back upstairs to my bedroom.

I left the lights on and also flipped on the small TV in my bedroom. Some noise would be nice, and keeping the house lit up made me feel less alone. I chose a home redecorating show to stream.

"28 episodes. Perfect." I said to myself. Then I climbed into bed with my leftovers, ready to face the night on my own.

Too late I realized I hadn't brought a fork with me from the kitchen. Too miserable to do anything about it, I flipped open the container and ate the cold Thai food with my fingers.

Pretty soon I was stuffed and I put the empty containers on my nightstand. Still no sign of Zak. Looking around my messy room and comparing it to the pristine newly decorated rooms on the TV, I was overwhelmed with sadness.

I flopped onto my back and threw my arm over my eyes, groaning. "I don't like this, Zak. If you're here I want you to show me that you're here." I peeked one eye out from under my arm.

Nothing was changed.

Yet absolutely everything was different.

I had always lived quite content on my own. Never feeling lonely. Happy to keep everything neat and tidy around me and keep myself healthy and well put together. Just the way I liked it.

Now my house was in need of a good cleaning, I was disheveled and distraught, and the only thing I cared about, the only thing I could think about, was seeing Zak again.

"He wouldn't leave without saying goodbye," I reassured myself, even as my throat tightened and tears swelled in my eyes. I tried to be positive. Maybe he had found a way to restore the balance and he was watching over me like he always had. I peeked out from under my arm again. "Is that it? Are you here and I just can't see you?"

There was no answer. I sighed and resigned myself to the possibility that there wouldn't be an answer. At least not tonight.

"Fine, I'm going to sleep," I told invisible Zak. "Can you figure out a way to let me know you're here and show me in the morning...please."

I pulled my comforter up to my chin and let the tears run down my cheeks as I fell asleep.

thirty-seven

Zak

To say I was waiting impatiently for Esme to appear would have been an understatement. I was practically jumping out of my skin. I only had a few hours before Elsie got back from her date and I wanted to be there waiting for her as me, Zak, a normal human man. Not an angel anymore.

"ZakZakiel. You're in a hurry?" Esme asked as she twinkled into sight right in front of me.

"I am. I've decided what I want to do."

Esme waited, one eyebrow raised in anticipation.

"I want to become human again."

Esme nodded, a slight lift of her mouth into a whisper of a smile made me think she was pleased. "And may I ask why you have made this decision?"

"I want another chance at it. Another shot at living a happy life."

"I see." Esme adjusted her glasses and leveled a sober look at me. "And you understand that you are giving up immortality. You will no longer have any supernatural abilities. You will go back into the world just as you are right now and from this day forward you will age, be subject to illness and injury, and have to make your way on your own without any assistance from me or any other supernatural forces?"

"Yes," I nodded, returning her look with equal seriousness. "I understand."

"May I ask why?"

I thought about it a second. A lot of why I was doing this was Elsie, but it was more than that. It was for me, too.

"I'm in love. With Elsie. All I want is to know I'm going to see her every day. That I'm going to see her smile, maybe make her laugh, watch her be brave and funny. And that I can be more to her than someone who looks over her. That maybe she could love me, too. Maybe, after all this time, I can live a life with meaning."

Esme looked at me thoughtfully. She turned slightly to her right and waved her hand through the air, bringing up an image as if we were watching a television screen.

The image was of Elsie in her pajamas, curled up on her bed eating leftovers out of a Chinese takeout container with her fingers. She looked tired and sad. Watching her pierced my heart with pain.

"This is who you want to give up immortality for?"

My throat grew thick with a knot of emotion. I had to clear it before I could respond. "Yes. That's her."

Esme studied Elsie for a moment and looked back to me. "Do you know if she loves you in return?"

I shook my head 'no'. Then, afraid that would make a difference, I held up my hand to stop Esme from telling me I couldn't become human. "But I would rather live my life with the chance of earning her love than not. I would rather face the reality of death if there's a chance I could win Elsie's heart."

Esme waved her hand and the image of Elsie disappeared. Her strong gaze looked straight into me, looking to see if I meant what I said.

I stood my ground and stared right back into her eyes, unafraid. "I don't want to be invisible anymore, Esme."

I saw the change in her eyes. A smile that started in them and grew until the corners of her eyes were crinkling and her mouth turned up.

My heart raced inside my chest and I felt instantly weightless. Light as a feather, which was pretty ironic considering.

"I can do it? You'll make me human again!?" I asked.

Esme's smile continued to grow. "Everyone deserves a second chance, Zak."

I let out a laugh. Zak. She called me Zak!

Esme chuckled too, then a short giggle escaped her lips. Not her normal tempered response.

Still elated, but curious, I asked, "What are you so happy about?"

"You've done it."

"Done what?"

"It was your life, Zak. Your life that you needed to find and value. It was your life that you were entrusted with and your life you had to make a positive difference in. You have found meaning in living. In connection. In Elsie. And it will only get better from here.

What a rush that was, to hear that I had done what I was supposed to. That I was on the right path, after all that time not knowing or understanding.

I clapped my hands and rubbed them together, anxious to get going. "When can we start this switchover?"

"We can start right away."

"Great, let's do it." I looked around at our rainbow light surroundings. "What do I do? Do I have to sign something?"

Esme chuckled again. "No, all I need is for you to tell me once and for all that you choose to be human."

"All right." I straightened my back and shook my arms out, loosening up like a prize fighter. Then, as clear as I could speak, I said, "Esme, I choose to be human."

The pain in my back was instant. I realized it must be coming from my wings. Hot searing pain like they were removing my wings with a blow torch. I squeezed my eyes tightly closed and took short shallow breaths to keep from crying out.

Esme's measured voice came to me. "There will be some discomfort during the transition, but don't be afraid. When it is complete you will be human again."

I blew several breaths out as the pain spread, encompassing my abdomen, chest, and neck. I had to bend half over to stay in an upright position. "How long does it take?"

"Not long, considering. However, I can't give you a precise number. It's different for everyone."

Surprised, I managed to open one eye enough to look at her. "You've done this before?" I moaned out loud as the pain reached the top of my head and stretched all the way to the bottom of my feet.

"Oh, my, yes," she said matter-of-factly.

Through clenched teeth I asked, "What's the longest it's ever taken?"

There was a pause, which I swear she did for effect, before she answered, "Three days."

thirty-eight

Elsie

Zak wasn't there in the morning.

I woke up to my alarm expecting him to be nearby, having forgotten his absence while I slept. But as I rolled over to hit the button and stop the incessant beeping I saw the almost empty Thai containers on my nightstand. Everything came rushing back.

I sat up, rubbing sleep out of my eyes. "Zak?" My voice was still froggy so I cleared my throat and called his name again, louder.

Nothing.

Hugging my knees to my chest, I tried to wrap my head around what had happened. I couldn't believe he had left me without a word. Without a goodbye. Without anything.

My face scrunched up. I wanted to talk myself out of crying. I wanted to distract myself with some other task. But I couldn't. I was overwhelmed with a throbbing ache in my heart and, suddenly, hot ugly tears streamed down my cheeks.

Using both hands to cover my eyes I wept bitterly, running our last conversation over and over through my mind.

He'd said it wasn't an emergency. He'd said nothing bad was going to happen. He'd said things were going to get better.

"You said you wouldn't leave me," I sputtered angrily, but it wasn't truly anger filling my soul. It was despair.

A bird chirped outside of my bedroom window, pulling my attention toward the dim pink light of sunrise. There was another chirp. Very close.

I scrambled out of bed and went to the window. As I approached I saw several small grey birds lined up on my window ledge, taking turns hopping back and forth, and cocking their tiny heads one way then the other.

Not wanting to scare them, I slowed down. As I got closer, the sun lifted on the horizon. More light shone on the window ledge and into my room. More birds landed on the ledge and even more were chirping underneath the window on the shrubs below.

Ever so slowly, I unlocked the window and raised it up inch by inch. The chirping filled my bedroom. I managed to poke my head partially out the window, just enough to get a glimpse of the shrubs in my yard, which were completely covered with the same little grey birds.

All at once they burst into the air, fluttering and zipping up past me into the morning sky. I knew it was a sign. I knew it was Zak.

With teary eyes I watched the flock of birds fly back and forth above the nearby trees before dispersing. Zak was with me. I was sure of that from the bird's presence. But I could no longer see him. My heart twisted in my chest. The hurt came on so fast and strong that I sucked in my breath.

A heaviness overtook my whole body. My shoulders slumped and my head drooped down. I couldn't look out at the beautiful morning, there was no joy in it for me.

Zak...my Zak...was gone. Gone back to be my guardian angel, yes, but erased from my life in the real world, probably forever.

It seemed such a cruel way to end things. After everything we'd been through together. Had he asked for it? Had he known it would happen like this? One moment he's there and the next, poof!?

Never again would he run into me accidentally with his massive wings, or tease me about my healthy cooking, or give me a sly smile when something struck him funny, or make up a weird light show for Amelia and Abe.

"Abe," I said, remembering the trip to Camp Morningstar for his 7th birthday.

I wiped the tears from my face with both palms and sniffled. I needed to get myself together for Abe's sake. For my sake. I glanced around the room, imagining where Zak might be standing, watching me fall apart. I couldn't decide where he was, so I spoke to the room as a whole.

"If this is how it's going to be then I guess there's nothing I can do about it. I wish you would have told me before you took off." I stopped the bitterness that threatened to rise in my voice and took a deep cleansing breath. "I shouldn't complain. I got my life back, right? And you got yours."

I turned and stalked into my bathroom to take a shower so I could get dressed and be ready to leave. Later, as I pulled clothes out of my dresser and shoved them into a duffle bag, I had one last thought for my now invisible guardian angel.

"You better be on your toes this weekend, Zak. Camp Morningstar has tubing and ziplines and even bungee jumping." I laughed a little as I thought about how he would react if I decided to go bungee jumping. "Now that our time together is done and I've worked out some of my problems, I'm a brand new person. And you know what, Zak? Nobody, not even you and your rainbow light supervisor lady what's-her-name, can predict what I might do."

thirty-nine

Zak

I came to face down on the floor of Elsie's kitchen. Fitting, I supposed. Whoever said the powers that be didn't have a sense of humor was wrong.

Whoever else said that changing from an angel into a human wasn't excruciatingly painful was also wrong. I could barely move. Every part of my body hurt.

My body.

I let out a laugh at the idea, but laughing hurt.

"Oh, God," I groaned, then rethought my wording. "No, never mind, I'm good. Don't worry about it. I'll be fine." Didn't want to step on any toes right away.

I pushed myself up off the floor, every muscle and joint screaming in protest. When I got to a standing position I felt weighted down, solid. No wonder, I hadn't experienced the pull of gravity on a human form for a while. I took a few steps, getting my earth legs back. It wasn't bad. In fact, it felt kinda good. Kinda strong.

Daylight streamed through the window. It was morning already? How long had I been transitioning?

"Elsie?" I called out.

There was no answer. The house was silent. I needed to go look for her, but I needed something else first.

"Water." I was so thirsty. Like a guy who's been lost in the desert kind of thirsty. I lurched my new earth legs over to the kitchen sink and turned on the faucet. Not waiting for a glass I shoved my head into the sink and drank cold, delicious, refreshing water until I couldn't drink anymore.

Straightening up, I wiped my mouth on the sleeve of my flannel shirt, noticing for the first time what I was wearing. Red flannel, jeans, boots, the same thing I'd been wearing for over a decade.

"I'm gonna have to get some new clothes." I smiled at that realization, but my good humor was short lived because I was hit with another forgotten sensation. Hunger.

Opening Elsie's refrigerator door, I scanned the contents and mourned the sight.

Celery. Something that looked like tuna salad. Oat milk. Bottled iced tea.

I muttered under my breath about falling in love with a dietician, but pulled all the food out and started eating anyway. I needed something in my gnawing stomach. It felt like I hadn't eaten in, well, ten years.

After polishing off the tuna salad in three bites I munched on some celery and searched through her cupboards. Once again, disappointment reigned.

Bran flakes. Gluten free crackers. Something called nutritional yeast, which I refused to touch.

Studying the bran flakes, I figured I could make them work with the oat milk. It was something anyway. That's when my eyes landed on the cookie jar.

Cookies.

With much trepidation I opened the lid on the jar and found

it chock full with, you got it, carob chip cookies.

"No," I moaned in protest, but my stomach was master of this moment and it needed food. My tastebuds didn't get a say in the matter. With a grimace I bit a piece off, chewing as fast as possible, willing myself not to gag. I managed to swallow and washed it down with a swig out of the oat milk container.

"Gah!" I shouted my disgust to the empty kitchen and looked at the ingredients on the back of the oat milk, as if knowing what was in the drink would help. It was awful, but it was doing the trick. The debilitating pains in my stomach were receding. I could find more appetizing food later. Right now, I needed to find Elsie.

"Elsie!" I yelled again. Still no answer. I grabbed more cookies and left the kitchen to look for her upstairs.

After a full search of the house I didn't find her. That's when I remembered that she was going to Camp Morningstar for the weekend. With Keith.

Suddenly, I realized I didn't know what day it was. I needed to figure out what day it was and find Elsie. And I needed to do all of that without a cell phone or any money to pay for transportation.

Or I could sit around her house eating carob cookies until she returned from Camp Morningstar engaged to Keith or something stupid like that.

"Not happening," I said to the empty house.

I recalled that Elsie kept spare change in a little glass dish on her dresser. I figured I could borrow that and maybe find a few coins in the cushions of her couch. I ended up with $4.79 in quarters, dimes, nickels and a lot of pennies in my pocket. I also packed up a clear plastic bag full of the remaining cookies, the box of gluten free crackers, and a bottle of iced tea then headed out the door to find a ride to Camp Morningstar.

Luckily, Elsie didn't live too far from the city center and I was able to walk there to look for a cab. Without a cell phone I couldn't get a ride share. I hoped I could find a cab that would take me as far as $4.79 would get me.

Several pedestrians caught my eye as I walked and said a quick 'hello' or 'good morning' as they passed. Not sure why I was getting so much attention, I double checked behind me to make sure I didn't still have wings. All clear. Then I realized that people were just being polite and that's what it was like to be visible. I warmed up to the pleasantries.

I happily said good morning back to several folks then finally worked up the nerve to ask one nice woman what day of the week it was.

In a friendly, yet cautious, tone, she answered, "Saturday."

"Great, thanks!" Saturday. Elsie was at Camp Morningstar. Now to find a cab.

I spied a cabbie parked outside of the downtown medical clinic who looked like he was taking a break leaning against his cab.

"Esme," I said under my breath as I walked across the street toward him. "I know I can't ask for assistance anymore, but I wonder if you could just send me a little bit of luck to get me on my way."

The cabbie was a big guy with a full beard, but kind enough eyes as he watched me approach.

"Morning," he said.

"Good morning," I started, nervously switching my clear plastic bag to my other hand. "I wonder if you could help me out?

The man's big brown eyes looked me up and down then he gave me a quick nod.

"Great, thanks. I need a ride, but I don't have a lot of money on me."

He smiled and chuckled, a deep, good humored sound. "I see. You're not from around here are you?" He had a heavy accent, though I couldn't have identified the country.

"Not exactly," I answered truthfully.

The cabbie eyed the carob cookies in my plastic bag and chuckled again. "I'll tell you what. I've got a little time and I haven't done my good deed for the day. So I'll give you a ride for a price you can afford."

"Okay, how much?"

He pointed at the cookies. "Are those homemade?"

"These?" I held up Elsie's cookies. "Yes, my girlfriend...well, the girl I'm trying to get to right now made them."

The cabbie's eyebrows lifted. "Ah, a romantic. Very noble. Then I'll give you a lift for some of those delicious cookies?"

"Deal," I said, trying to forget that they weren't exactly delicious cookies.

"Get in." He swept his arm toward the back door of the cab.

Excited about his offer to help me, I completely forgot about being a human with no supernatural powers, and walked directly into the door of the cab without opening it.

"Whoa, my brother, what are you doing?" The cabbie asked, helping me up off the ground.

"Sorry, I wasn't thinking."

He gave me an uncertain look. "You really aren't from around here, are you?"

"No, I'm not," I admitted sheepishly.

"They don't have doors where you're from?" he asked, amused.

"I'm kinda preoccupied."

"Come on then, no time to waste." He opened the back door for me and closed it carefully after I got inside.

I handed him the bag of cookies as soon as he got in, keeping the box of crackers and iced tea with me. Maybe I was in luck and he wouldn't try one of the carob cookies before we got to our destination.

He started the cab and pulled into the street. "So where are we going?" he asked, opening up the bag and taking out a cookie.

I winced, but tried to act natural. "Camp Morningstar. Do you know where that is?"

He took a big bite of cookie and chewed a couple of times before his expression changed from one of delight to disgust. He looked at me in the rear view mirror, his heavy brow lowering and pinching together. He managed to swallow then took several gulps out of a travel mug.

"Your girl made these?" He asked, eyeing the bag of cookies next to him with suspicion.

"Yes."

"You sure you want to find her, my brother?" He caught my eye in the rear view mirror and laughed at his own joke. "Just kidding, love is blind and, apparently, can't taste. I know, I know."

"Sorry, she's a dietician. They're healthy cookies. Carob instead of chocolate," I admitted.

"That's the problem is it?" He grinned. "Maybe I will give them to my wife. She likes to stay healthy. Well, now, where was it you needed to go?"

"Camp Morningstar," I answered, relieved Elsie's carob cookies weren't going to get me kicked out of the cab.

He clucked his tongue several times in dismay. "That's all the way in Summer Springs, my brother. A two hour drive. I can't take you that far today. I have a family to feed you know."

"It's that far?" I slumped back in the seat, not sure how I would ever get there. "I understand. Thanks anyway."

Still watching me in the rear view mirror, he must have found me as pitiful as I felt, because the next thing I knew he said, "What I can do is take you to the bus station. You can get the next bus up to Summer Springs. They might even have one that goes right to Camp Morningstar."

"Really? Oh, man, that would be great, thank you."

"How much money did you say you had?" The cabbie asked.

I swallowed, embarrassed to admit it. "I've only got $4.79 in change."

The cabbie chuckled again, the same rumbling good natured laugh. "All right, then. I'll take you to the bus station and get you a ticket for Summer Springs."

"You will?" I was floored by his willingness to help a stranger.

"I know, I know, I'm a saint." He said, still chuckling as he steered the cab around a corner. "That must be why my mother named me Angel, yes?"

I followed his gesture to the cab license in full view on his dashboard. It showed a picture of him smiling widely for the camera and right next to it, clear as day, was his name, Angel Adebayo.

"Thank you, Angel," I said. Then, under my breath I added, "And thank you, too, Esme."

forty

Elsie

By the time we reached Camp Morningstar I was deflated. Completely hollowed out. Numb to all emotions...except sadness. But a person can only be sad for so long. I was burned out on sad, so I became fully numb instead.

I had managed to pack up my car, pick up Keith, and get to Brooke's house at the pre-determined time. Since it was my family vacation I had insisted on using my car. Halfway to Summer Springs I regretted that decision. It was all I could do to keep up with following Brady and Brooke ahead of us and hold my own in a conversation with Keith.

Finally, I gave up on the conversational part. I figured it was more important that we not get lost or in an accident on our way to Camp Morningstar. Keith eventually stopped trying to talk to me and amused himself with watching the scenery out the passenger window.

We arrived late morning and set up camp. I managed to do my part in getting lunch ready, but I didn't have an appetite.

"Still have an upset stomach, my sweet?" Keith asked, sidling up to me while I was methodically putting together cold chicken sandwiches for the group.

My sweet? I narrowed my eyes and pursed my lips, not sure I liked that term of endearment. Or if I was open for any term of endearment.

"Hungry?" I pushed a chicken sandwich into Keith's hands, putting a barrier between us, and questioned the wisdom of inviting him along. I wasn't in the mood to rebuff awkward romantic advances during our stay at Camp Morningstar.

"When is Zak coming?" Abe asked.

"Oh, he's here," Brooke answered, giving me a wink.

"Where?" Abe and Amelia both looked around hopefully.

Brooke gestured toward their tent. "Right over there by the tent."

Not seeing him, they turned to me instead of their mother. My heart sank. Poor Abe. He wasn't going to have Zak at his birthday party.

I put my hand on the top of Abe's head and gave him a sympathetic look. "I'm sorry, buddy. Zak couldn't come."

"What are you talking about? He's right over there." Brooke motioned toward the tent again, giving me a 'stop screwing up Abe's birthday weekend' look.

"No, he's not, Mom," Amelia told her mother firmly. She put her arm around her brother's shoulders for consolation. "How come Zak can't be here, Aunt Elsie?"

I knelt down to their level and looked into their sweet little faces. "I'm sorry, you guys. Zak had to go back to where he came from."

"To heaven?" Amelia whispered.

I nodded. "Yes, but he's still watching over us I'm sure."

Abe straightened his back, putting on a brave front. "Will he be with Great Aunt Millie?"

A knot filled my throat and made it so I couldn't speak. I nodded, fighting back tears.

Abe looked like he might cry for a moment, but instead he sniffled and nodded his head quickly. "That's good. I don't want her to be lonely."

"Me either," I managed to say and gave them both a big bear hug.

When I stood up, Brooke was still displeased with me for not going along with her pretending to see an imaginary Zak. To avoid that conversation, I asked Keith if he wanted to walk around the camp and look at the activities. He did.

We followed wooden signs pointing up a wide dirt path, which promised to take us to the Summer River bridge, the bungee jumping site, the ziplining course, and a special training area where they taught rock climbing. As we walked, the silence between us grew large and unmanageable, but I wasn't in a place to break it.

Keith finally did.

"I get the feeling that you may be regretting inviting me on this family trip."

His words made me flinch, but I couldn't deny their accuracy. I stopped walking. "I'm so sorry, Keith. You're exactly right. You're always exactly right about everything, that's why I don't understand what I'm feeling."

"And what are you feeling, Elsie?"

I pressed both of my palms against my cheeks and let out an uncontrolled moan. "I can't believe I'm going to say this...but I don't think I have feelings for you."

Because I can't stop thinking about my guardian angel who was in my life for a while, but now he's gone and my world has fallen apart since he left, I wanted to add. But didn't. Instead I watched Keith absorb what I had said, calm and collected, as always.

"I see," he rocked back on his heels and looked at the dirt path between us for a few seconds before lifting his eyes to mine. "I can't say that I'm surprised, but I am disappointed."

"Oh, Keith, I'm so sorry. I shouldn't have led you on and kept going out with you if I wasn't sure. I just...I just..."

"You were in shock and in mourning for your lovely Aunt Millie." He took my hands in his and squeezed them affectionately before letting them go. "I don't feel led on at all. That is what we do, right? We reach out to people and spend time with them and see if they are a good fit. And if not, no hard feelings."

"No hard feelings?"

"None at all." Keith looked around the beautiful wooded area where we were walking. "Are you still interested in seeing the sights? Perhaps going ziplining? I've been looking forward to the ziplining."

I let out a little laugh. "I don't know if I'm in the mood for ziplining, but I'll walk with you if you want to check it out."

Keith did want to check it out and when we arrived he was excited to give it a try. "You sure you don't mind?"

"Of course not, zip away," I tried to make a joke.

Keith turned his attention to a fit blonde who was greeting people and signing them up for their zipline experience. She was pretty and had really, really white teeth. During the sign up process they became quite chatty and seemed to be having a good time together. I decided to leave him in her competent hands and go see the bridge. More power to them.

"Well, Zak," I said quietly as I walked alone. "I guess it's just you and me now."

Filled with a sense of relief knowing I was no longer navigating a relationship with a man I couldn't drum up feelings for, I was intrigued by the Summer Bridge. It was a beautiful bridge built for foot traffic floating high above Summer River.

I walked out onto the bridge and leaned against the heavy wooden railing, a shiver moved across my shoulders. The river roared underneath me. The Summer River was one of the widest rivers in the area, deep too. The water rushed quickly below the bridge, churning over on itself, creating its own rapids.

I was happy in a way. Content to be on my own, knowing

that even though I couldn't see him, Zak would always be nearby. I found some comfort in that.

And I was grateful. Grateful for the time we had spent together and for everything he had done for me. Before I knew Zak I would never have been able to stand on a bridge this size and look down at the water without having major anxiety.

"See?" I said softly. "It wasn't all for nothing." I let out a sigh that was a mixture of hope and sadness. I still had hope for my future, but would forever wish for one more moment with Zak. One more time I could feel his arms wrap around me and hear the sound of his voice.

Several shouts and a long, loud scream erupted from the center of the bridge. A small crowd of courageous adrenaline seekers were gathered at the bungee jumping station located there, cheering on one of their own who had just taken the leap.

With nerves buzzing in the center of my stomach, I made my way to the station to watch the others take their turns. Soon I was captivated by the process. Watching each jumper prepare with the guides, build up their courage and wait for the bungee guide to say "Jump!" Then simply push off into the air.

What might it feel like to totally let go and trust that everything would be okay? The buzzing in my stomach moved through my entire body and covered my skin with goosebumps.

I wondered, too, why I was still afraid. I was luckier than most. I knew without a doubt that I had Zak looking out for me. There was no reason for me to fear anything in life, not even jumping off a bridge.

Knowing he would be with me, probably have his arms wrapped around me the whole way down, made the idea less and less terrifying by the second.

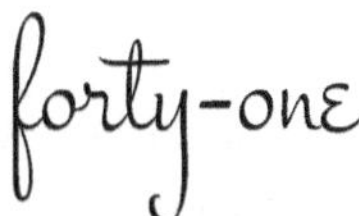

Zak

I got off the bus at Camp Morningstar thankful for the help of strangers and wistful over my lost ability of flight. Riding a bus was rough, especially when you haven't been operating within the confines of full gravity for a while.

Still, I was there. I had made it. I took in a deep breath of fresh air and stretched, scanning the area. I was in a parking lot full of cars. Four different dirt roads led up from the parking lot into the wooded area toward campsites and activities. I had no idea which road Elsie and her family had taken.

"Well, better get started," I said to myself, taking off toward the road furthest to the left. I would work my way left to right and hope for the best.

"Yo, Zak," Jacob, the guy I'd been sitting next to on the bus all the way to Camp Morningstar called out to me. I turned around. "You want a ride?" He motioned to a convertible jeep that was picking him and his two other friends up.

"Sure, thanks," I said, hopping into the only open spot in the back. At least I wouldn't have to walk the entire camp to find Elsie.

About ten minutes later the jeep came to a stop at their camp-site. I hadn't seen any sign of Elsie or her family during the ride up. I got out and thanked them for the lift then took off on foot.

In the near distance I could hear the sound of a river. There were occasional shouts of fun and excitement both from the river and the zipline course I was passing. I craned my neck to see if Elsie was ziplining, but didn't spot her.

As I trudged along, my stomach started up again. I had reluc-tantly polished off the gluten free crackers on the bus ride, but that wasn't going to keep me full for long. Apparently I had the appetite of a growing hippo since becoming human again. It didn't help that as I moved past campsites the tantalizing smell of food being cooked on an open fire filled the air. My stomach rumbled.

I was debating if I had the nerve to approach one campsite that was having a hotdog cookout for about a dozen people when I heard a familiar voice.

"Zak! Zak!"

I whirled around seeking the owner of the voice and spied Abe running toward me, followed closely by Amelia.

I crouched down and opened my arms wide. "Abe! Happy birthday, buddy!"

They both ran straight into me, hitting my chest hard like little kids do when they're happy to see you. I grabbed them into a bear hug, standing up as they squealed in my arms.

"Zak! We thought you wouldn't come!" Amelia said.

"How could I miss Abe's birthday party?" I asked, twirling them in a circle before putting them down.

"Aunt Elsie said you were up in heaven with Great Aunt Millie," Abe said.

"She did? Well, I was for a while then I came back to hang out with you guys." I looked in the direction where they had come from. "Where is your Aunt Elsie?"

"Come on, Zak!" Ignoring my question, Abe took one hand and Amelia took the other. "Come see our tent!"

Just then Brooke emerged from their campsite looking for her kids. When she saw them holding my hands, she squinted suspiciously.

Before she had a chance to demand an explanation, Amelia spoke up, "Mommy, Zak came to Abe's party!"

Dumbfounded for a few moments, Brooke simply stared as we approached. When we reached her she managed a confused, "Zak?"

I nodded in greeting. "Nice to meet you. You must be Brooke." I couldn't help but chuckle at her surprised stare as the kids led me past her to their campfire.

Brady was tending the fire and stood up when Abe and Amelia led me to it. "Hello," he greeted me with a watchful eye.

"Honey," Brooke called out as she hurried to join us. "Honey, this is Zak...Elsie's friend Zak." She gave her husband a meaningful look.

Brady's eyebrows shot up. He looked me over more closely then let out a lighthearted laugh. "We didn't think you were real."

"No, Daddy," Amelia disagreed. "We said he was invisible. We didn't say he wasn't real."

"Oh," Brady looked politely confused. "Pardon me."

I reached out to shake Brady's hand. "Sorry for the confusion. I'm both visible and real, as you can see."

"Yes, yes you are," Brooke commented as I shook hands with her husband.

"So, is Elsie here?" I asked, glancing around the campsite.

"Not right now. They should be back any minute..." Brooke's voice trailed off, uncertain what to say. "Are you hungry? We have some chicken sandwiches that didn't get eaten at lunch."

Tapping one loose fist against my chest I gave her a slight bow. "Thank you, I am really hungry, actually."

Pleased that she could do something to fill the social awkwardness, Brooke brought me a sandwich. Taking a larger bite than I should, I closed my eyes and groaned with pleasure as I chewed.

"Delicious," I tried to say.

Amelia giggled. "Don't talk with your mouth full, Zak."

I nodded in agreement and continued to make apologies with my face while devouring the chicken sandwich. Brooke and Brady looked on, still confused, but slightly less alarmed.

Someone walked up behind me and stepped around to join the others. Keith.

"Keith," Brooke said his name as if she was announcing it to the world. "Um, this is Zak. Elsie's...friend."

Keith gave me a friendly nod. "Nice to meet you, Zak."

I had a mouth chock full of chicken sandwich so all I could do was mumble, "Hey."

"Where's Elsie?" Brooke asked Keith.

"Oh, she didn't want to do the zipline. I saw her walking toward the bridge. I thought she would be here by now."

A pang of worry went through my gut. Something about what he said didn't sit right. As soon as I was able to swallow what was in my mouth, I excused myself.

"I think I'll go look for Elsie," I told Brooke.

Concern crossed her face. "Do you think something's wrong?"

"No, not at all. I'm just...I just want to tell her I'm here."

Brooke watched me leave with her brow furrowed, holding Abe and Amelia's hands so they didn't come with me.

I followed the signs for Summer Bridge with a growing sense of urgency. Maybe I was being overprotective, but what Amelia had said kept running through my mind. Elsie had told them I went to heaven with Aunt Millie? I didn't like the sound of that.

As soon as the bridge came into view, my stomach lurched. There, standing on the edge of the bridge, a good 50 feet or more above a rushing river, was Elsie talking animatedly to the bungee jump crew, getting her harness fitted.

I started jogging toward the bridge. Then broke into a run.

"Elsie! Elsie!" I shouted. She didn't look in my direction.

I reached the bridge running so fast I had to grab hold of a post to round the corner. The bungee guide was yanking on Elsie's harness and backing her up to the edge. He held the bungee rope in one hand. It hadn't been hooked to her harness yet.

My legs flew underneath me, yet I wasn't covering ground fast enough. Fear filled my chest as I shouted again, "Elsie, no!"

She looked up, confused at the sound of her name. Then she locked her eyes onto mine, recognition filling them.

I reached the group of people surrounding her, pushing my way through. "Elsie..." I was out of breath.

She beamed at me. "You're back!"

"Yes, I'm back."

"You've been hiding," she laughed with delight, but was still standing dangerously close to the edge. "Where did you go?"

"It's a long story." I reached out my hand toward her. "I'll tell you. Want to come away from the edge so I can explain?"

She laughed again, glancing behind her at the drop off into the water. When she looked back at me, her eyes were shining with excitement. "No, Zak. I'm going to bungee jump! Can you believe it!?"

She shuffled her feet back a few inches closer to the edge. My heart leaped into my mouth and I froze. I had never felt ice cold fear coursing through my veins. It rendered me helpless. I glanced down at the bungee guide, who still hadn't attached the rope to her harness. Why wasn't he grabbing her and pulling her away from the edge?

"Almost ready," the guy said.

"Thank you, Henry." Elsie grinned at him then raised her beautiful sparkling eyes to me.

"Elsie, you can't–" I started.

"Yes, I can. I'm not afraid! Can you believe that?"

I took a step toward her, not wanting to move too quickly and cause her to react and fall off the bridge.

"You're making me a little nervous standing so close to the edge like that," I said.

Elsie laughed again. "Don't be silly. You're here, right?"

"Yes, but–"

"And you promised me you'd always have my back."

"Yes, I will. But you don't–"

"Don't jump, Elsie," Henry instructed from where he was kneeling in front of her, bungee cord in hand.

She sucked in her breath and looked at me with bright eyes. I knew instantly that she hadn't heard him correctly, but it was too late.

I lunged forward to grab her as she raised her arms up to the sky, but I wasn't fast enough.

"No!" I shouted.

Elsie threw herself backwards off the bridge with no bungee cord attached to her harness.

Henry leaped forward and reached for her, but he came up short. His arms flailing through empty air.

She was gone.

I did the only thing I could do.

I jumped after her.

forty-two

Elsie

Rushing air. Blue sky. Bright sun.

They consumed my senses as I flew off of Summer Bridge.

Joy filled my heart even as it pounded wild and free in my chest. Zak was here with me. He was back. I was not going to have to face my life without him.

I had never felt more alive.

Suddenly, Zak was flying next to me, grabbing my arms and pulling me roughly into his chest midair. Not quite the easy floating sensation of flying that I expected, but maybe he was enjoying the sensation of plummeting toward the raging river below as much as I was.

He held me tight, wrapping one arm up and around the back of my head so my face pressed into his flannel shirt. I noticed he didn't smell like funnel cakes. He smelled like...a man. Musky, a little sweaty, and kind of like chicken with mayonnaise.

We turned in the air so he was below me. At any moment I

expected the bungee rope would stop our rapid descent. Or Zak's wings would spread out and bring us to a pillow soft landing before the rope even had a chance to yank me back up into the air.

Neither of those things happened.

Zak held me fiercely and we kept falling. There was a slight buoying feeling, as if a sudden wind had blown up from the river and slowed our fall. We floated, but only for an instant, before smashing into ice cold water.

I couldn't take in a breath. It was no longer air that rushed and swirled around me, it was the wide, deep river. Zak was gone, ripped away when we crashed. There was only freezing water and the realization that I was being swept away.

How had this happened? Why hadn't the bungee rope, or Zak, kept me safe above the rolling, frothing river?

I couldn't think about it. Couldn't think about anything except frantically finding the surface so I could catch a breath of air. I had zero control over which way my body flipped and tumbled in the water, but managed to take in a deep breath each time my head bobbed at the top for a few seconds.

Miraculously, I found myself sputtering and coughing, washed up on the bank of the river. I had just enough strength to pull my body out of the rushing water before I collapsed on the rocky shore.

I heard coughing and choking behind me and flopped over far enough to see Zak climbing out of the river's current and crawling up next to me.

"Elsie, are you all right?" He was out of breath, his soaked clothes hung off of him and his wings...were gone.

"What happened to your wings!?" I asked, alarmed.

He shook his head, still gulping in air.

"Oh my God, Zak," I pushed myself up off of the ground, a little unstable on my feet and whirled around to look up at Summer Bridge. People on top were screaming and shouting at us. I turned back to him. "Did we just fall off a freaking bridge!?"

Zak got up, brushing rocks and dirt off of his wet hands. "Well, technically we jumped off the bridge."

"But why didn't the bungee cord stop me?"

He took in a few more jagged breaths, steadying himself before answering, "Because you weren't connected to the bungee cord yet. That's what I was trying to tell you."

I stared at him. Something was wrong. His wings were gone and he looked...different.

I gasped in horror. "Did we just die!? Are we dead!?" I pressed my hands against my chest and stomach and sides, checking for what I wasn't sure.

He coughed out a laugh.

I looked around at our surroundings. "It's weird. Not what I would think it would be like."

"What?"

"Being dead."

"You're not dead, Elsie."

I narrowed my eyes at him. "How do you know?"

"I know, okay."

I wasn't convinced. "You don't have your wings anymore. And...and you don't smell like funnel cakes."

"So?"

"Maybe you're dead, too. Can that happen?"

"I'm not dead either. I'm human."

I was almost as surprised at that admission as I had been at the idea of us being dead.

"You're human? What are you talking about?"

He closed his eyes, dropped his chin to his chest, and took in a deep breath before looking up at me again. "This isn't exactly how I was going to tell you."

I swayed a little on my feet. The shock of what had just happened and of Zak talking crazy was getting to me. "Whatever you're trying to tell me, just tell me."

He moved in front of me and took my hands in his. They were warmer than mine, but his skin was still cool and wet with grit stuck to it. I looked down at my hands, which were also covered with dirt and small rocks. My hands were shaking.

"I was given the chance to become human again. So I took it."

I gaped at him. "You're not an angel anymore?"

"Correct."

I pulled one hand out of his grip and pushed against his chest a few times. He felt like a real human, though he had always felt mostly human to me when I had touched him.

I blinked several times, trying to understand. "I thought you had gone back to being my normal guardian angel. You know, invisible."

"Nope, I went to Esme to become a human." He threw out his hands as if presenting himself on a game show, but with a touch of sarcasm.

A new, more terrifying, thought hit me. "I've been alone all this time?"

He shifted his weight back and forth on his feet. "Well, yes, I didn't know it was going to take that long. I thought it was going to be, like, an instant thing."

"I thought you were watching over me," I said, reeling from the new information. My knees wobbled. "I could have died!" My eyes grew wide as I looked at where his wings used to be. "*You* could have died!"

His face softened and he looked at me steadily. "I didn't die and neither did you." Then he added, "I was watching over you. I still am. Only in a different way."

"Why?" I asked.

"Why?"

"Yes, why? Why would you become human?"

Zak looked into my eyes. Raising his hand to my cheek he brushed off some grit that was still stuck there, then cupped my face. He smiled shyly and when he spoke his voice was a little unsteady, "I'm in love with you, Elsie. I wanted to be human so we had a chance to be together."

A thrilling tingle raced through my entire body, leaving me

speechless. I stared up at him, not believing I had heard him right, unable to grasp all of his words at once.

After a few long moments, Zak's face fell, his hand slipped from my cheek. "That's not something you wanted to hear?"

"No, no, no," I grabbed his hand in mine and held it against my chest. My heart was beating so hard I was certain he could feel it. "I just didn't know that was a possibility." I laughed, loud and sudden.

Zak hesitated, confused by my reaction. "Is this too much for you?"

"Too much? No!" I put my hands firmly on his shoulders, feeling his honest to goodness, solid, human body under my fingertips. "You're real? This is real?"

"Yes, it's real," he said firmly. Then, more uncertain, "Is it what you want?"

Warmth radiated through my chest. My heart overflowed with joy, filling me up so fast I was shaky. My wobbly knees gave way and I started to drop to the ground. Zak caught me and held me against him. I was in his arms and I never wanted him to let go.

My bottom lip trembled as I put my palms on his cheeks. "Zak, of course it's what I want. I love you."

His smile, which I had seen often, was something other-worldly that day. Like sunshine straight from heaven it sank into my soul.

He bent down and pressed his lips to mine. The strong, warm, gentle kiss of a real live man. I was no longer on solid ground, I was soaring.

Sirens sounded from the bridge. There was more shouting, some of it closer, arising out of the woods next to the river. They were coming to get us after our bizarre bungee jumping accident.

We both looked up to see a crowd gathering on the bridge. I recognized Brooke, Brady, and the kids immediately. Brooke was waving both arms and screaming hysterically.

"We're okay!" I waved at her. I turned to Zak. "She's freaking out."

Zak eyed the height of the bridge. "Well, it was a miracle that we made it."

I turned back to him. "Why did we make it? Shouldn't we at least have broken bones or something?"

A sparkle of rainbow light appeared in the nearest grove of trees and a small woman with short white hair, glasses, and huge white wings with gold tips stepped onto the rocky beach.

Zak grinned. "Esme, I knew that was you slowing us down at the end."

She smiled mischievously. "Not exactly me." She turned her attention my way. "Hello, Elsie. It's wonderful to meet you."

"Hello, Esme," I answered, more in awe of her presence than I would have expected, given I had spent so much time with angel Zak. "I've heard a lot about you."

Esme's smile widened. "And I, you."

Another figure walked out of the sparkling rainbow light and stood next to Esme. I sucked in my breath and covered my mouth with my hand. Zak's arms gripped me harder so I wouldn't collapse.

"Aunt Millie!" I could barely say her name before I burst into tears.

It was Aunt Millie, looking healthy and beautiful, beaming with joy at me and Zak.

"I wanted tell you that I'm all right, Elsie. I'm happy. And I want you to be happy, too. All of you," Aunt Millie said.

Zak squeezed me gently and I managed to stop crying. I looked up at him and back to Aunt Millie. "I am happy, Aunt Millie. Very happy."

"So it's all worked out okay," Zak declared with some measure of relief in his voice.

"It has." Esme smiled at him then at me. At us. "You two have good balance between you."

Zak laughed. "Balance! That's what we've been after, isn't it?"

Esme nodded serenely and clasped her hands together with

satisfaction. The light surrounding her and Aunt Millie grew brighter, taking them back to where they had come from.

Right before they disappeared, Esme gave us a wink. "And don't worry too much, kids. Even though you can't always see us, we've got your back."

The End

about the author

Cecil LaTwine resides in the deeply wooded lake country of Michigan. She loves nature, legends, myths, and all things pertaining to the possibility of magic. She has two grown daughters, three dogs, and a cottage sized house, which she adores.

With a particular affinity for dogs, large and small, a deep desire to befriend the crows who visit her property, and a secret wish for the power of flight, she has always been drawn to magical and supernatural stories.